“Ho[illegible] your ha[illegible]” Adam asked.

Joanna gave him a little one-shoulder shrug. Gesturing to her wrapped hand, she said, “Takes two hands to braid it.”

He reached for his jacket and slipped free the string that ran through the casement of the hood. “This ought to do the trick.”

She straightened and presented her back to him. Slowly he reached out and gathered the heavy mane in his hands . . . and the fascination began again.

Her hair was like nothing he'd ever touched before. Soft as down, fragrant as an autumn morning, it seemed alive with an energy of its own. He couldn't help it. He sifted it through his fingers, combed it away from her neck, held the weight of it in his big hands. The experience was an artful seduction of his senses, sensual and slow and impossible to fight.

“It's beautiful,” he murmured raggedly, tempted to bury his face in the spun gold. With more determination than skill he tied the mass together at the nape of her neck. “How's that?”

She stood very still, her shoulders tense with emotion. “Much better, thanks. It was getting hot,” she answered quietly.

He felt her shiver despite her comment. His body responded with a burning warmth of its own. Too aware of the heat, he dragged his gaze from hers, only to have it snag on the slender column of her throat. Her skin was delicate. His hands were not. Yet he ached to touch her there, to press his lips to her softness, taste the salt and sweat and sweetness of her. . . .

WHAT ARE *LOVESWEPT* ROMANCES?

They are stories of true romance and touching emotion. We believe those two very important ingredients are constants in our highly sensual and very believable stories in the *LOVESWEPT* line. Our goal is to give you, the reader, stories of consistently high quality that may sometimes make you laugh, sometimes make you cry, but are always fresh and creative and contain many delightful surprises within their pages.

Most romance fans read an enormous number of books. Those they truly love, they keep. Others may be traded with friends and soon forgotten. We hope that each *LOVESWEPT* romance will be a treasure—a "keeper." We will always try to publish

LOVE STORIES YOU'LL NEVER FORGET
BY AUTHORS YOU'LL ALWAYS REMEMBER

The Editors

Cindy Gerard

Slow Burn

BANTAM BOOKS
NEW YORK · TORONTO · LONDON · SYDNEY · AUCKLAND

SLOW BURN
A Bantam Book / June 1992

If you would be interested in receiving protective vinyl covers for your Loveswept books, please write to this address for information:

Loveswept
Bantam Books
P.O. Box 985
Hicksville, NY 11802

ISBN 0-553-44175-2

Published simultaneously in the United States and Canada

Bantam Books are published by Bantam Books, a division of Bantam Doubleday Dell Publishing Group, Inc. Its trademark, consisting of the words "Bantam Books" and the portrayal of a rooster, is Registered in U.S. Patent and Trademark Office and in other countries. Marca Registrada. Bantam Books, 666 Fifth Avenue, New York, New York 10103.

PRINTED IN THE UNITED STATES OF AMERICA

OPM 0 9 8 7 6 5 4 3 2 1

Dedication

To my sister, Wanda Burrows, who was around during the conception of this baby. And to my editor, Elizabeth Barrett, who stuck with me through a difficult birth.

To the good people of Lake Kabetogama I apologize for rearranging your beautiful lake. It was not a question of improving on perfection. I love Kabby just the way she is. The plot, however, demanded a few changes.

And to Debbie Sheets: Thanks again, friend. I owe you.

Slow Burn

One

She recognized a stray when she saw one. The man limping down the pine-needle-covered path toward her, a beat up duffel bag in one hand, definitely had the look of a stray.

Shoving back a bothersome wisp of burnished red hair, Jo kept him in her sights as she worked a rope through the pulleys on the boat hoist.

He was tall, she noted, and well put together, even though he leaned toward the slim side. And despite his pronounced limp, her first impression was that he was laden with attitude—a rebel attitude that would have made her wary if first-hand knowledge hadn't told her what it was hiding. Vulnerability was a trait she recognized all too well, though she'd choke on the word before she'd ever admit ownership.

That surprising and telling glimpse into his character intrigued her far more than it should have. She couldn't afford to be curious. She needed to be concerned. Not many strangers wandered into the lodge this time of year. None had ever walked in who looked like this one.

He wasn't a Northlander. From his too-long-to-be-respectable, wind-tousled blond hair, to the worn bomber jacket hanging open over a dark T-shirt and equally lived-in jeans, everything about him said trouble. She'd bet her dwindling bankroll he wasn't a potential client. Shady Point Lodge attracted retirees or vacationing family men who found a week or two in the wilderness of northern Minnesota a pleasant escape from the nine-to-five grind and city smog. This scowling stranger, who looked like he'd rather wrap his hands around the throttle of a Harley than around a fishing pole, stood out like the proverbial sore thumb.

As he drew nearer, however, and his striking, elementally male features came into sharper focus in the early autumn dusk, Jo realized this man would stand out anywhere.

And, she concluded on another flash of insight, he was a restless, troubled man. A man in pain. Not just physical pain, as evidenced by his labored steps, but emotional. Though his stoic scowl was the stamp of a loner and invited nothing but avoidance, she sensed a loneliness in him . . . a loneliness that might rival her own.

Stunned and shaken that she'd drawn yet another parallel between them, she pulled back quickly. Careful, Taylor, she cautioned herself, not fully understanding what it was about him that sparked her unprecedented interest. He was just another stray. She'd do well to remember that stray dogs have a tendency to bite. Instead of standing there trying to armchair analyze him, she should be heading for the boathouse and the twenty-gauge shotgun she kept loaded with bird shot for those occasions when she needed to run off a pesky bear.

The truth was, though, she was too tired to move.

"I do *not* need this today," she muttered under her breath, and turned her energy back to the boat.

But Jo had learned long ago that what she needed rarely equated with what she got. That was why it didn't surprise her when she planted her feet on the dock and gave the rope a hard tug, that it jumped off the pulley. The leaky boat she'd been struggling to hoist out of the water for the better part of an hour skidded back a foot. She swore roundly and succinctly.

Cooper, who until that moment had been sleeping in the grass a few yards away, woke up with a start. The chocolate labrador lurched to all fours. The coarse hair on his broad back bristled to attention when he spotted the stranger. Jo could have kissed his bushy hide for putting things back into perspective. Cooper, at least, had the good sense to bare his teeth and issue a low warning growl.

The man stopped in his tracks. His gaze snapped to Cooper, who, bless his canine heart, was playing protector to the hilt.

"Something I can do for you, mister?" she asked, tying off the rope. Wiping her hands on her hips, she faced him with business-like brusqueness, intending to insulate herself against the unsettling effect he had on her.

The eyes that met hers with such piercing intensity only heightened the tension. They were a deep slate-gray, the color startling in its clarity. Diamond-hard, heavily brooding, they barely veiled an inner turbulence that made her think of the lake during a storm: Wild, reckless, volatile.

"For starters, you can tell that dog to back off."

His voice, she wasn't surprised, matched his eyes—hard-edged and ominous.

Though it took some effort, she met his stony look without flinching. "Cooper won't bother you if you don't bother him."

"And if I don't bother you, right?" he said, his attention returning to the dog.

"And if you don't bother me," she confirmed with more assurance than she felt. Attack dogs and family-vacation resorts simply didn't mix. Any minute now she was certain Cooper's growl would give way to a doggie grin. The hair on his back was already losing its starch, and she suspected the effort it took to keep his tail from wagging would soon get the best of him.

She moved up beside Cooper as if to hold him back. "If you've got business here, I'd suggest you state it."

He squinted against the reflection of the setting sun glinting off the lake. "It would be a lot easier to talk, kid, if I was sure he wasn't hungry and I wasn't on his menu."

Kid? Jo gritted her teeth and bit back an oath. She forgot that she was tired and that for a moment she'd been moved by the sadness in his eyes. Forgot, even, that she should be wary. She glared at him, considering whether to give him fair warning that at this moment he was in more danger of being attacked by her than by her dog.

She should be used to it by now. At the ripe old age of twenty-six she had no delusions about her appearance. Joanna Taylor was plain. Her features were pleasant at best, giving her a street-urchin innocence that would undoubtedly prompt leery bartenders to card her until she was forty.

Her skin was fair but bore mercifully few freckles, which would have her look more like the Raggedy Ann she felt she resembled. Oh, the curves were all there, but by no stretch of the imagination would they ever be described as lush. Hard work kept her body lithe and compact. That was the way she wanted it. But, damn, she got tired of being called kid!

She would have been less offended if he'd mistaken her for a man. She worked like one, swore like one, and looked . . . like a kid, she finished dismally as she mentally assessed her navy boxer shorts, strictly business T-shirt, and the single thick braid of hair she'd tucked under a cap that boasted SHADY POINT LODGE above the bill.

So what did she expect? His reaction to her was typically male. Men either wanted to play big brother with her or treat her like one of the guys.

But this man wasn't a typical male. Though it galled her to admit it, her response to him wasn't one bit typical either. She was attracted to him. Unaccountably attracted. She'd taken one look at his dark, angry scowl and recognized the need in him. That he hadn't bothered to see if there was more to her than met the eye, too, was a blow to her pride—and further proof of just how tired she was.

Get a grip, Taylor, she ordered herself. Drawing herself up to her unremarkable height of five feet two inches, she let the Indian summer breeze that whispered off the lake clear her head. But her ire rose again when Cooper added insult to injury by giving up his pretense of watchdog.

The pup sliced her a slow, guilty look, then with his tail wagging shyly, lumbered over to the stranger and accepted a pat from his large hand.

Traitor, she accused silently.

Glaring at the dog and at the man, Jo finally realized why he was there. He must have seen her ad.

"If you came about the job," she began, not bothering to hide her irritation, "I'm really not sure you'd be up to it." She glanced at his bad leg before making a sweeping gesture over the twelve dilapidated log cabins and the main lodge. "As you can see, this place needs a lot of work."

Cooper—the miserable mutt—had switched allegiance completely. He was on his back at the man's feet, squirming like a beached whale and begging for a belly rub.

"I'm not here about a job," he said, wincing as he bent to accommodate the wallowing dog. "I'm trying to find Jo Taylor. They told me at the Crossroads Store to look here."

Jo's wariness returned in a heartbeat, and with it, her anger. Her experience had been since she'd moved back from the Cities that spring that when someone came looking for her by name, it was usually because he'd gotten wind that a Taylor had plans to reopen the lodge. Generally he came with a bill in hand. An old bill, one of many her father had accumulated and then run out on when his drinking had stressed the resort's finances. She'd been sixteen when it had finally gotten the best of him and he'd simply disappeared.

Now she understood. This guy was just another bill collector. And to think she'd— Well, it didn't matter what she'd thought. Feeling even more foolish for her sophomoric reactions to his rebel good looks and brooding eyes, she sighed in resignation.

"So what's the bad news?" she asked.

His head came up. His gray eyes questioned.

"Anyone comes looking for me by name, I figure it's bad news. And if you think I'm going to be surprised by the fact that you want money, think again. It's become a way of life."

He straightened slowly, his look as doubtful as it was perplexed. "*You're* Jo Taylor?"

"Last time I looked." She answered his dubious scowl with an affronted snort. "Sorry to disappoint you."

He shook his head. "No, it's not that. It's just that I was expecting . . ." His voice trailed away as she whipped off her cap, and her thick auburn braid uncoiled and fell heavily down her back.

For what seemed like an eternity, she endured his silent, measuring stare. Her cheeks burned with both the heat of anger and a devastating sensual awakening as his gaze tracked the length of her bare legs, the curve of her hips, and finally the shape of her breasts, which were unbound beneath her thin cotton T-shirt.

Brutally aware of her shortcomings, she straightened her shoulders and said defensively, "You were expecting a man?"

"No," he stated bluntly as his gaze crawled back to her face. "A woman."

Adam Dursky watched in considering silence as the girl—damned if he could think of her as anything more—drilled him with a look that could have blistered paint.

So this little green-eyed roughneck with a boy's body and fire-engine-red hair was John Taylor's daughter.

He took a longer look, one she met with defiance, and hoped she was as tough as she wanted him to think she was. She needed to be tough. What he'd come to tell her wasn't going to be easy to take, not by any man or woman's standards.

He shifted his shoulders, feeling uncomfortably out of his element. Dark alleys and city streets were familiar territory. They ran in sync with the ugliness of hoods flashing switchblades, or strung-out junkies waving Saturday night specials. But here, with the clear air scented of pine and facing a fresh-scrubbed, wide-eyed kid . . . hell, it just didn't match the dirty job at hand.

Before he saw it through, though, he had other needs to attend to. He had to get off his leg. It was burning like a blue bitch. He'd been lucky to hitch a ride from International Falls as far as the county road. But the hike from the main road to this backwoods lodge had been pushing it.

He stripped off his jacket. "Mind if I park on that bench for a minute?"

Her expression cooled a bit as she considered that, then she indicated with a negligent, one-shoulder shrug that he could suit himself.

Her attitude confirmed what he'd already suspected. She was a brat. That fact just might make his job easier to stomach.

Nothing, however, was going to make it easy to move. Bolts of fire ripped through his thigh as he stepped toward the cedar bench. He swallowed back the nausea that accompanied the pain. Clenching his teeth, he eased down.

When the worst had passed, he raised his head to see her working the devil out of the handle of an old pitcher pump. A jolt of heat shot through his lower body as he watched her trim little butt bounce to the rhythm of her pumping arm.

Whoa, he told himself, stung by his unexpected reaction. You've been on your feet too long, Dursky, if a tomboy like her can set your blood simmering.

Refusing to accept the unsettling sensation for what it was, he discounted it as another warning that he'd over done it. He shook it off, only to be knocked off balance again by the concern in her eyes when she handed him a tin ladle.

The water felt good going down, and almost as good as being off his feet. Wiping his mouth on the back of his wrist, he nodded his thanks and, for reasons he couldn't explain, quickly looked away.

"He puts up a good bluff," he said gruffly as the naturally friendly Lab curled up at his feet. "But he'll never make it as a watchdog."

When he met her eyes again they had, thankfully, turned as cool as the water.

Leveling the same agitated look on him as she had the pup, she crossed her arms over her chest and leaned back against the pump. "Loyalty doesn't seem to be his strong suit either. But I'm sure you're not here to talk about dogs. You came looking for me so you must have business. I'd appreciate it if you'd state it and let me get back to work."

He had business all right, messy business. Now that the time was at hand to deal with it, he wished he was back in Detroit.

He avoided both her pinched frown and the inevitable by checking out the lodge. In its day, it could have been something. By John Taylor's accounts, it had been *more* than something. He supposed if you looked past the disrepair of the buildings and the general deterioration caused by years of brutal winters, some people would see a certain rustic appeal in the log cabins. All he saw, though, was a shambles.

The lake, however—and he admitted this grudgingly—was intriguing. So was the surrounding forest that somehow managed to grow out of a rock-studded landscape, then blended to shades of gray at the water's edge.

Lake Kabetogama. How many times had he listened to John go on about his beloved Kabby, his lake of rough waters and glacial blue skies? And about his daughter, Jo, who was the light of his life, his sweet little princess who he'd reluctantly left with his sister in Minneapolis when he could no longer give her what she needed.

Adam met her eyes again and suddenly felt very old and uncomfortable confronting this woman/child, who was more pauper than princess and about as sweet as alum.

Hell, just look at her. She wasn't any bigger than a minute and appeared to be made up of mostly unruly red hair and big green eyes—*impatient* green eyes, he corrected himself—that complemented what she'd already shown him was a testy nature.

She wasn't a raving beauty, not in the classic sense at any rate. But neither was she plain. When weighed individually, her features weren't striking. But her full lush lips, strong cheekbones, and a nose that could have defined the word 'pert,' all blended together into an intriguingly, if not exotically, striking face. A face that announced innocence and insolence in bold-faced letters, and pride with a capital P.

He supposed that if a man chose to look past that pride and her prickly disposition, he'd find a fiery woman underneath, a woman worth pursuing—if a man had a penchant for pursuit. Which he didn't, Adam assured himself as he assessed her slight, compact figure one more time.

Dragging his gaze back to her face, he reminded himself that she was John's kid, and John was one tough old bird. Every indication was that the apple hadn't fallen far from the tree. If he was certain of one thing, it was her moxie. She'd need plenty of it if she was going to make a living from this run-down resort.

As if reading his thoughts and taking grave exception to them, she met his stare in kind. *I'm tough*, she said without uttering a sound.

Yeah, brat, I know you are, he answered silently. And he was glad to see that she could fight her own battles since there didn't appear to be anyone around to fight them for her.

"Your business, Mr. . . ."

"Dursky," he said, knowing he couldn't put it off any longer. "Adam Dursky. I'm a friend of your father's."

She didn't flinch. She didn't even change the tempo of her breathing. But something flashed in her eyes—surprise, pain, maybe even anger—at the mention of her father, and he knew he had her attention.

She pushed away from the pump. With long, purposeful strides, she walked back to the hoist and untied the rope that suspended a sixteen-foot motorboat half in, half out of the water. When the rope stuck then slipped again, she let loose with a string of obscenities that would have made a biker blush.

He rolled his eyes skyward. Lord, she was a piece of work. Why he felt compelled to help her when she'd clearly like to spit in his eye, he didn't know.

Shaking his head, he limped to the hoist and slowly but forcefully pried the rope from her hands. Like the rest of her, her hands were small but strong. When he accidentally brushed one with his own, she snatched it away as if he'd burned her. He felt the burn, too, and decided it would be wise not to wonder at the reason.

In edgy silence, she let him maneuver the rope through the pulleys while she guided the boat into the cradle and secured it a couple of feet above water level. As they worked together, he couldn't help but approve of her grit, and of the way she moved with an economy of motion that was swift, sure, and efficient. And of the way her hips sweetly filled the confines of her wash-faded shorts.

He nodded at the boat. "That's a nasty hole," he said, ending a silence that had become too heavy and a fascination that was growing too strong.

She poked at the gouge in the boat's hull, breaking away the rough edges. "This lake is full of rocks. Every once in a while, you hit one. It's going to have to dry out before I can do anything about it."

She turned and walked over to a building that could have been a pump house or a bait house. He couldn't tell and really didn't care. All he could think about as he watched her was, *As tough as she is, she's running now. She suspects why I came and she doesn't want to hear it.*

Well, dammit. He didn't want to tell her, but he hadn't traveled all this way just to leave without seeing it through.

"Look . . ." he began, wishing he'd never left Michigan. "I guess there's no easy way to say this."

She uncoiled a garden hose and flipped a switch on an antiquated electric pump that began noisily drawing water from the lake. "Then why don't you just say it?"

Careful of the uneven ground, he limped up behind her and watched as she rinsed down the dock. "Your father is very ill. He's in a hospital in Detroit."

The silence stretched so long, he'd begun to think she hadn't heard him. Then in a very tight voice she said, "I'm afraid you've wasted your time, Dursky. I don't have a father. My father died a long time ago."

Without meeting his gaze, she shouldered past him and walked to the pump house.

"Are you telling me you're not John Taylor's daughter?" he asked when it became apparent she wasn't going to elaborate.

Her slight shoulders stiffened. She let out a tired breath, flipped off the switch, and began rolling up the hose. "What I'm telling you," she said, measuring her words, "is that I was thirteen when my mother died. It wasn't long after that my father decided to die too. He drowned himself in as many bottles of Southern Comfort as he could find."

Adam knew the story. He'd heard it all from John, had listened more than once as John had poured out his guilt and his regret. Avoiding her eyes and the pain he knew he'd see there, he looked out over the lake. He did *not* want to get more deeply involved in this. He'd come as a favor to John, to deliver a message, and then he was going to leave.

Only he knew he couldn't leave. Not yet. Not with those wounded eyes asking him for answers that would make sense of John's senseless and wasted life.

"He speaks of you often," he said, forcing himself to look at her.

Her eyes flared with anger before they clouded with hurt. "Does he? Does that mean he told you how he dumped me on an aunt who didn't want me, and promised to come back for me? Did he tell you how he let this place—my home—go to ruin? How the only memories he left me are attached to an endless string of bill collectors?"

Jo stopped suddenly when she realized how much she'd revealed. Pinching her eyes shut, she swore. Then looking everywhere but at him, she pulled herself together. "He shouldn't have sent you here."

If she'd really written her father out of her life, Adam thought, his news wouldn't be bothering her. Realizing that, he pushed a little harder. "John didn't send me. Coming here was my idea. I thought you might want me to take you back to see him."

Her stubborn eyes told him she *did* want him to, but she wasn't going to admit it. Back in her tough-guy role, she just shrugged as if to say, "Well, you thought wrong, buddy."

She was a hard case all right. He really needed this, but he had no one to blame but himself. Disgusted that he'd ever conceived this stupid idea of coming to find her, even more disgusted that he was letting her get to him, he made one final, ruthless effort. "It makes no difference to you that he may not make it?"

The anguish that information obviously caused

her was almost her undoing. And his. He'd meant to get her attention, not cut her to the bone. He'd accomplished both.

Her silence was as long as it was tense. When she spoke, her voice was brittle with the effort to conceal emotion. "It's like I said. As far as I'm concerned, my father is already dead."

If he'd seen any indication that she'd give in, he would have pressed it. Angered by her stubborn pride but accepting her decision, he shrugged. "It's a real shame no one ever taught you how to be direct, kid." Her face was as void of feeling as her voice had been until he added, "Or how to forgive."

She paled, then blinked hard. Hugging her arms tightly around her waist, she spun away from him and looked out over the lake. "Good-bye, Mr. Dursky."

He studied her stiff back and gave up. "Yeah. I guess it is."

Telling himself he was relieved to wash his hands of her, he gave Cooper a farewell pat on the head and snagged his jacket and duffel. He was halfway up the drive, damning her pride, his own stupidity, and his bothersome leg in equal measures, when he heard her call his name.

"Dursky . . ."

He stopped and turned to face her. She looked as tentative as if she were about to pass her hand over a flame.

"Have you got a car parked up there?" she asked finally and with such guarded hope, he knew she wasn't going to like his answer.

"Nope. No car. I hitched a ride."

The oath she muttered was short and concise. The scowl she gave him was a dandy. "Then you aren't going anywhere tonight."

"Come again?"

Looking disgusted but resigned, she sighed heavily. "I said, you aren't going anywhere. You'll never catch a ride back to the main road this late, and up here you don't want to be on *any* road after dark."

"Bears, city boy," she explained when he frowned. "They own these woods. Within half an hour of sunset, there'll be more of them on the pavement than there are cracks. And you'd be a pleasant change of menu from the nightly fare down at the dump."

Her mouth thinned to a grim line, she shut and locked the bait house. "Cabin number one is in pretty good shape." She pointed vaguely toward the cabin closest to the lakeshore. "You can spend the night there. Give me half an hour to clean up and I'll throw together a meal."

When he just stood there, she planted her hands on her hips and answered his scowl with one of her own. "Look, I don't like it any better than you do, but neither do I want to spend the rest of my life with *yours* on my conscience. The sad fact is that I'm stuck with you. Don't mistake this for hospitality, because it's not."

"Hospitality?" he muttered under his breath as he watched her turn on her heel and head for the main lodge. "The thought never crossed my mind, Red. It never crossed my mind."

But another thought had, he realized as his gaze traced what was beginning to be a familiar and pleasant route up the length of her slim, sleek body. A disturbing thought. He was relieved he had a reason to stay . . . which implied he really hadn't wanted to go . . . which suggested he was a little more intrigued with that little redheaded waif than was either warranted or wise.

Two

Stretching his good leg out on the cabin's deck railing later that night, Adam laced his hands behind his head and stared across the vast, murky satin of the lake.

Were it not for the water lapping in a soft, hypnotic cadence against the wooden pilings of the dock, and a bit more aggressively against the outcrop of stone lining the jagged shore, the quiet would be deafening.

The darkness was absolute. As he sat there soaking it all in, his thoughts kept straying to the girl. Jo Taylor. Joanna. The redheaded Rapunzel with the little-girl face and the sailor's mouth.

Her meal had been hot and filling; her company tolerable but distant. He had to give her credit. She knew how to mind her own business. And, he'd decided, she was every bit as tough as she appeared.

Dry-eyed and efficient, she'd set about settling him in and making sure he had the necessities to get through the night. Her father was not mentioned again. Well, that was fine with him. No hysterics, no sloppy show of emotion. She didn't want to admit she had feelings for him, didn't want to go see him. Fine. Coming here had been a long shot and it hadn't worked out. Tomorrow he'd be gone. Morning couldn't come soon enough to suit him.

He'd intended to be on the road before sunrise, but she'd made a believer of him about the bears when she'd carefully wrapped and then stowed the supper's garbage in a locked storage shed. At first light, though, he was out of there. Then he could forget about her and this place.

The longer he sat in the darkness, though, the more apparent it became that he wasn't going to forget either soon.

There was an eerie, almost ethereal element to the north country that was at once compelling and repelling. Compelling was its beauty, stark, serene, unspoiled. Repelling was its isolation and the diminished sense of self-significance amid the fathomless depths of the water and the magnificence of a seemingly endless sky.

And then there was the woman. He was still having difficulty with her. She was a little girl by appearance, and a seasoned survivor of the school of hard knocks by necessity. But she was a hard-head by choice, he suspected, and surprised himself by fighting a grin.

His grin faded when he envisioned the defiance so evident in her emerald-green eyes. Some man needed to show her that there was more to being a woman than simply being a survivor. Some man needed to make those eyes shine with a different kind of fire. The fire of desire.

She'd be a tiger in bed, he mused, as fierce in the giving as in the taking of pleasure. Unbidden, his body reacted to a picture of pale limbs bathed in moonlight, of small breasts quivering to a man's touch, of a sleekly muscled body arched amid tangled sheets and a silken curtain of red hair. Yeah, he decided, trying to distance himself from that picture and the fire it created in his loins. Some man needed to show her . . . but it wouldn't be him. It damn well couldn't be him.

The unexpected creak of her screen door opening and closing snapped his head around. Statue still, he listened to the crunch of her footsteps as she walked down the rocky path to the lake. Then he saw her in the night, and he realized he'd been waiting for her.

Her slim dark silhouette skimmed like smoke through the shadows and rekindled that swift, intense heating of his blood. An explicit wanting. A profound sensual awareness.

She's a kid, for Pete's sake, he reminded himself angrily as she sat cross-legged on the weathered boards of the dock and stared out across the water. Not your style, Dursky. Not your speed. And in this life or any other, she was not an option.

He clenched his jaw. Knowing he should leave, yet feeling compelled to stay, he watched Cooper, his dark coat catching a hint of starlight, amble up beside her.

She thought she was alone and appeared even more childlike than she had in the daylight as she draped an arm over the Lab's nudging shoulder, then linked her other arm around his chest.

Something inside him tautened, knotted, when she buried her face in the dog's thick fur. Leave now, Dursky, he ordered himself coldly, sensing what was about to happen. She was not his problem. And she was not his cure.

Yet his heart was pounding heavily, his throat felt oddly constricted as he listened to her first muffled cry.

So the tough little nut had a crack after all, he mused, wishing it had come as a bigger surprise. Wishing he didn't have to fight the urge to go to her.

•

Closing his ears to the sounds and his mind to the proof of her vulnerability, he rose and limped soundlessly into the cabin.

In the darkened bedroom he lay down, reminding himself that in the morning he'd be gone. The next day Jo Taylor and Shady Point Lodge would be nothing more than a memory. Her tears were not his concern. And for the hundredth time, she was *not* his problem.

And neither was it a problem that he felt her pain and her loneliness bone-deep and compared it to his own . . . or that for the first time in a very long while he fell asleep wondering if the bottom of a bottle of bourbon was still an appealing sight.

During all those years Jo had spent in the Cities, her homesickness for Kabetogama and Shady Point had always been at its worst in September. Autumn was her favorite time of year in the North country. Besides the glorious colors, there was something about the air—the crispness, the scent of falling leaves, and in the mornings the nippy promise of winter—that made Kabby unique to any other place she knew.

This morning, however, chin-deep in lake water that was running a chilly sixty-four degrees, she found herself wishing fervently that it was the middle of July. And wishing that she could quit thinking about Adam Dursky.

It wasn't that she'd expected him to tell her good-bye or anything before he left, she thought as she breaststroked away from the dock, heading toward the skittish mallard that was helplessly trapped in the water some thirty yards out.

Dursky had done her a favor by slipping quietly away early that morning. She was glad she hadn't had to face him, glad he was gone. It was just that . . . Just what, Taylor? she asked herself, fighting an unwanted sting of disappointment. Just that you'd wanted to see him one more time?

No. She hadn't wanted to see him again, she told herself firmly, then shuddered from the continued shock of the icy water. He was a loner with an attitude, nothing but trouble. She didn't want to think about him anymore, or about the memories he'd stirred up about her father. What she wanted was to keep her mind on what she was doing so she wouldn't end up drowning right along with the duck she was determined to save.

"Easy, big guy," she cooed through chattering teeth as she drew nearer to the frightened drake. "You poor thing. You're exhausted, aren't you, baby?"

Trussed up like a Christmas goose, trapped in yards of fishing line, the drake would die a slow, cruel death if she didn't get to him and set him free.

"I know you're scared and I know you're pooped, but if you had let me get you from the rowboat earlier, we'd have had you untangled by now. And I wouldn't have icicles for legs and come out of this with a cold that'll probably last until Christmas."

Very slowly, so as not to spook the exhausted greenhead, she swam a little closer, talking and soothing all the way.

"You've got to let me at you, big guy. If you bob around out here much longer without food, you know you're going to starve to death. That is if some big ole northern doesn't swim up under you and have you for his dinner first. And what would that sweet little lady of yours do then, huh?" She glanced over her shoulder at his mate who was circling them with a watchful eye. "You think she wants to make that flight south the end of the month all by her little lonesome? Of course she doesn't."

Teeth still chattering, she drew within five yards of the frightened drake. Any second now he would panic. If she didn't get to him in time, he'd drowned himself and maybe her right along with him, if she was unfortunate enough to get tangled in the line too. Mallards weren't big, but they were tough. Even though this one was worn-out, she knew he'd have some major league fight left in him.

Sucking in a big breath, she submerged. Swimming the final five yards underwater, she surfaced inches from the startled drake.

Luck was on her side. Fatigue made his reaction time slow. She slung one arm around his back, effectively clamping his flailing wings to his body.

Working fast, she removed her knife from the sheath strapped to her thigh, sliced through the water, and cut the line.

It was obvious to her now what had happened. Some hapless fisherman had snagged his line on the rocky lake bed. By the time he'd realized he'd caught a rock instead of a fish, his line had broken—but not before several yards had spun off the reel. The lightweight monofilament line had pooled at the surface. When the unsuspecting mallard swam by, he'd become tangled.

Darn good and tangled, she realized as she worked to free him. He'd pitched and dived and rolled so many times, he'd ensnared himself even worse than she'd originally thought. She was going to have to swim him back to shore to finish the job. That was unfortunate for more reasons than one, the most bothersome being that his number one squeeze had apparently decided her mate was in danger. The hen was readying for an attack.

"I don't want your man, sister. Just lay off until I get him unwrapped. Then you can have him all to yourself."

Rolling onto her back, Jo cradled the wriggling mallard against her chest. Knowing that her own fatigue would soon become a factor, she kicked with all her might and headed for shore.

It was not an easy trip. Between the drake pecking and fighting and the hen dive-bombing her from all directions, she wasn't sure she was going to make it the last twenty yards.

As she went under a second time and surfaced choking, she came the closest she ever had to admitting it would be nice if sometimes she had someone to help her.

The next thing she knew, someone was.

A strong arm gripped her from behind and lifted.

"What the—" Dodging the slippery mallard's persistent bill, she craned her head around. "Dursky?"

"Got it in one." Gruff from exertion, his voice was deep and gravelly next to her ear. A rush that had as much to do with gladness as it did with surprise put all her senses on red alert.

"I thought . . . I thought you were gone," she managed to say, fighting her feelings and his strength as he wrapped an arm under her breasts and pulled her up snug against him.

"And I thought you were too smart to try to get yourself drowned. Now be quiet. Just hold still and enjoy the ride."

"Enjoy the ride? Dammit, Dursky, what—what do you think you're doing?"

"I'm saving your scrawny little neck, Red. And you're in no position to squawk, so for Pete's sake—Ouch! Would you quit squirming? Just hold the hell still, kid, and let me paddle you to shore."

"Kid?" she choked out through another mouthful of lake water. "Why you macho . . . Neanderthal . . . jerk!" She reared back in an attempt to break loose. When she came close to losing the duck instead, she reconsidered, just as she'd reconsidered that she was glad to see him. "I don't need your . . . help! Now let . . . go . . . of . . . me before we both . . . drown."

"The only one in danger of drowning here," he gritted out between labored breaths, "is you." If possible, he tightened his grip even more. "And I'll hold you under myself if you don't quit fighting me. Like it or not, you need help, so dammit, be still."

She didn't need his damn help, she thought. But because he sounded like he meant it and because he was physically stronger than she, she did as he ordered. She really didn't have much choice. Going limp in the water, she let him tow her to shore.

Long minutes later—minutes in which she was far too aware of the strength of his broad forearm wrapped tightly over her breasts, and of the hard resistance of his hip pressed against her bottom—his feet found purchase. Only when her own feet were planted firmly beneath her did he loosen his grip.

Winded, half-frozen, and as skittish as the duck in her arms, she jerked away from his steadying hand. Telling herself she was trembling because she was cold and mad, not because every pulse point where their bodies had touched was tingling with awareness, she stumbled across the rocks to the shore, leaving him thigh-deep in frigid water.

"You're very welcome," he grumbled as he slowly picked his way behind her.

"I did *not* need your help," she snapped over her shoulder, whipping her wet hair out of her eyes. "I was doing just fine. And don't expect me to dry you off because I've got my hands full with this bird."

"Well, don't put yourself out," he said in that

bluntly sarcastic way that seemed to come as naturally to him as scowling. "I'll just blow dry."

She spun around ready to level him with another barb. The sight of him standing there soaking wet, his arms spread wide, shivering like a soggy scarecrow in the crisp September breeze, brought her up short.

So the hood had a sense of humor. If she hadn't been so mad, she might have found him funny. But she *was* mad and, darn it, he *wasn't* funny. He was infuriating . . . and he was supposed to be gone. Which brought up the obvious question: Why was he still there? And why, no matter how hard she tried to deny it, wasn't she more upset about it?

Dodging the first question and denying the truth about the second, she hurried up the steps to the boathouse. The sound of his labored footsteps climbing the steps a minute later had her heart jumping again.

"There're beach towels just inside the door." She motioned with a jerk of her head toward a cabinet on the wall. "I'd suggest you grab one and make use of it."

"Your concern overwhelms me," he said, that same understated sarcasm oozing from each word.

"My only concern is for this duck," she lied, "and for the fact that I don't have enough liability insurance to cover a hospital bill if you get pneumonia."

Even as she found space on the cluttered workbench to set the duck down, she watched from the corner of her eye as Adam limped inside. His leg had to be killing him, she thought, not only from the exertion, but from her. She clearly remembered kicking and connecting under the water. Well, it was his own fault for surprising her, she reasoned. She hadn't asked for his help. And she hadn't needed it.

Shaking off the twinge of guilt, she listened to him shuffle around looking for the towels. When he found them, he draped one over her shoulders.

She didn't want to be affected by his gesture, or by the feel of his large hands, which had gently squeezed then lingered a moment on her shoulders before he reached for a towel for himself.

She riveted her attention on the duck. "There's corn in that plastic bin. If you would scatter it on the ground by the steps, it might lure the hen in. When the drake sees she feels safe here, he might eat a bit before he takes off. He'll need all the strength he can muster."

She had her hands too full of ruffled duck and her stomach too full of butterflies to worry about whether he took offense at her orders. It wasn't until he came back through the door, an empty corn scoop in hand, she realized he hadn't.

Then she did something else she didn't want to do; she looked at him. She was unable to stop herself from noticing the way his dark T-shirt and wet jeans molded to lean, hard muscle and a tall, rangy frame. And the way the lake water had darkened his hair to a dusty honey and combed it back from a face that consisted of angles so dramatic, they could have been carved from stone. Sinfully thick lashes clung wetly together over pewter eyes . . . eyes that still reeked of attitude and tried to reinforce the suggestion that there was no softness inside.

Yet there was softness. He obviously had a soft spot for her father, and he'd just shown one toward her. It had been no small effort to swim out into the lake and drag her in. And what manner of man would come all this way to bring her bad news?

To further confuse her, as he stood there in his

bare feet and goose bumps, she caught another fleeting glimpse of that vulnerability he worked so hard to hide. She wondered, as she had a better part of the previous night, at the cause of it.

Straighten up, Taylor, she ordered herself as she studied his whipcord lean torso. He was about as vulnerable as a grizzly, and probably just as dangerous.

So she'd found his rebel-without-a-cause look attractive yesterday. Today it was annoying. At least she tried telling herself it was. Dismally aware that she had failed, she forced her mind to business. "I could use your help here."

"Ouch," he said, measuring her request with those hard eyes of his. "I'll bet *that* hurt."

"Cool your jets, Dursky. I'm not asking for myself. It's for him. The less time it takes to free him, the better his chances for recovery."

He limped over to the workbench and picked up the wire cutters. With a deep scowl and surprising care, he snipped at the yards of knotted line. "How'd this happen to him anyway?"

As they worked together, she filled him in, telling herself that the sound of a soothing voice was for the duck's benefit, not hers. She also told herself that every time their fingers brushed together she didn't feel a tingling awareness of him as a man, and that the gaze that too often strayed to hers wasn't filled with the same kind of awareness.

"Fortunately," she finished, forcing lightness into her tone, "this doesn't happen too often. But when it does, most aren't as lucky as this guy. You usually find them after it's too late."

He gave a derisive snort. "I'd say it's a safe bet that most people wouldn't risk drowning for the sake of a duck."

"I did *not* risk drowning," she ground out, bristling at his lecturing tone. "I couldn't just ignore what was happening. This lake belongs to him. He shouldn't die due to a hazard created by man. It goes against all the laws of nature."

She made another mistake then, and looked at him once more. The questions she saw in his eyes were articulate and accusing. Without uttering a word, he changed the subject to that of her father.

And what law of nature, his eyes asked, *makes it right for you to turn your back on John when he needs you? How can you care so much about one lost mallard and ignore your own father?*

Stung by a guilt she didn't want to feel, she turned away. She didn't want him to guess that the puffiness around her eyes that morning had less to do with her near-disastrous swim than with the tears she'd shed for her father the night before. For all he'd once been. For all she'd needed from him that he hadn't given because he hadn't been around. For all he needed from her now that she couldn't make herself give.

Avoiding Dursky's piercing gaze, she shook off the guilt and concentrated on the drake. "I think that does it. Come on, big guy, let's see if your lady is waiting."

It was tough, trying to steady the frightened mallard with unsteady hands, but somehow she managed. She carried him outside, let him see his hen pecking at the shelled corn, and set him carefully at her feet.

Squawking at his first taste of freedom in several hours, the drake tested his wings, then waddled regally to his mate and joined her, feeding hungrily.

Jo leaned against the doorframe and watched them. Dursky, it seemed, was content to watch her. When she couldn't ignore his brooding stare any longer, she grabbed hold of the towel around her shoulders and faced him.

He was studying her as if he was trying to figure

out what made her tick. Or he was wondering whether it would be a good idea to throw her back in the lake, like some fish that was too small to keep. But as his gaze roamed her face and connected with her eyes, his expression changed. A look that was dark and dangerous and as charged as summer lightning sent her pulse racing.

No man had ever looked at her like that. The woman in her recognized it just the same. It was hunger, raw and real. It was need, naked and new.

Her heart slammed against her rib cage as she watched a startling combination of anger and desire transform the gun-metal-gray of his eyes to a deep smoky silver.

Stunned, telling herself she was only imagining it, she quickly averted her eyes. Her gaze fell on his duffel and leather jacket by the boathouse steps. She wasn't imagining them—or the fact that he was still there.

Fighting the sinking sensation in the pit of her stomach, she turned back to him and confronted the issue head-on.

"I thought you'd left," she said.

Once again, his face was hard and unreadable. "I thought I had too."

Whatever she thought she'd seen in his expression a moment ago was long gone. Chilled by the look that replaced it, she hugged the towel closer. "So why didn't you?"

He gave her a throwaway shrug. "Beats the hell out of me."

A tense few seconds passed before he tore his gaze from hers. He looked out over the lake, then took in the run-down cabins in a slow, critical sweep. "You said something about an ad for help. It's obvious that you need it."

Uncertain if she understood his meaning, her heart did a quick rolling tumble. "Don't tell me you're applying for the job?"

He cocked a brow, flashing his damnable attitude. "I might be. Don't worry about it," he added, reading her mind when her gaze strayed to his leg. "I can handle it."

Recognizing his indisputable dominant nature, she doubted there was much he couldn't handle. Except her. He wasn't going to get the chance. She'd make that clear right now.

"Let me get this straight," she said, regaining some of her composure. "You're telling me you want to work for me?"

He gave her another one of those long, slow looks that set her senses tingling. "Much as I'll probably regret it, I guess that about sums it up. It's a cinch you can't handle things by yourself."

The man had an uncanny ability to test the range of her emotions to their outer limits. Snapped from sensual awareness to anger in one fell swoop, she dragged the towel through her hair and considered slugging him. A strategically placed fist in that washboard-lean belly might not do much damage, but it would give her a great deal of satisfaction.

"I don't believe I've ever had anyone try to convince me to hire them by insulting me first. It's a unique approach, I'll give you that."

Again he shrugged. "I call 'em like I see 'em. A spade by any other name is still a shovel and this place is one hell of a mess. You need help, kid. I can provide it."

She stiffened, then counted to ten. Was it accident or insight that prompted him to push the right button to send her into a steaming rage? Wishing some of the fire she felt inside would radiate to her frozen limbs, she wiped her face on the towel and wondered if her lips had turned blue.

"I can't pay much more than room and board,"

she said, deciding to do some testing of her own.

He didn't bat an eye. "Money's not a problem."

Realizing that he was serious about the job, she tested him further. "Well, it's a problem for me and if you don't need it, there really isn't much incentive for you to stick around when the novelty wears off."

His eyes could have quick-frozen fire. "One thing you need to know about me, Red. I always finish what I start."

Do you? she wondered. And do you know what you might be starting by staying here? Shivering and knowing it wasn't just because she was cold, she tried again. "You don't strike me as the handyman type."

"Let's just say the work suits my purposes for the time being."

"Then let's also say I'd like to know what your purposes are. If you're running from some kind of trouble, I don't need it following you here. I've got enough of my own."

A muscle in his jaw worked. "No trouble," he said tightly.

No trouble? Oh, he was trouble all right. Yet she believed him. Some intangible, gut-level instinct told her she had nothing to fear from him. At the moment, however, doubting him was her only defense. Defense against what, she wasn't quite sure . . . unless it was the fact that she suddenly found herself more afraid that he'd leave than stay.

She'd wondered more than once what kind of a man he was, what had brought him there in the first place when a phone call would have accomplished the same thing. And why now, just as inexplicably, was he proposing to stay and help her?

Her hesitancy seemed to make him impatient.

"Look, you need help. I need something to do to pass some time for a month or so and I don't want to do it in the city. It's as simple as that. Now do I have the job or don't I?"

She met his challenging stare with one of her own, then surprised them both with her answer. "Yeah, you've got the job."

He nodded as if she'd just agreed that it was a nice day, instead of the equivalent of jumping out of a plane without a parachute. "Cabin number one suits me fine," he said, bending to pick up his gear.

"Fine," she echoed. As he walked toward the cabin, she realized she needed to regain control of the situation and called his name. "Hey, Dursky . . ."

He stopped and turned. A straight, wet lock of hair fell recklessly over his forehead and into his eyes.

She ignored the little ripple that eddied through her chest, and dug in her heels. "For the record. I'm on a deadline here or I wouldn't even be considering this."

He slung his duffel over his shoulder and his weight onto his good leg. "Translated, you don't really need my help so I shouldn't get to feeling indispensable."

For some reason she wanted to smile. She didn't. "You got it."

He turned to go again.

"Oh, and, Dursky . . ."

He faced her with an impatient sigh. "Yeah?"

She lifted her chin and stared him straight in the eye. "You call me 'kid' one more time and I'm going to find that shovel you were talking about and pound you into the ground with it. Are we clear?"

His grin was as disarming as it was unexpected. "Yeah, boss lady, we're clear."

She was still trying to deal with the tickling sensation in her stomach and the watery feeling in her knees that his smile had triggered, when Cooper came trotting out of the forest. The Lab skidded to a stop when he spotted Dursky. He sniffed the air, let out a welcome bark, then bounded toward him, all wagging tail and wiggling hips, as happy to see him as if he were a piece of prime steak.

"Miserable, unfaithful mutt," she muttered.

Shivering, she walked to the main lodge to shower and change into dry clothes. It wasn't until she was warm and dry again that what she'd done sank in. She'd just saddled herself with another stray. He was a rebel and a loner and the last thing she needed to complicate her life.

Adam. She rolled his name around in her mind, thought of the way his hard muscled body had felt molded against hers in the water, of the way his eyes had darkened when he looked at her.

Damning herself for the direction her thoughts had taken, she quickly braided her hair and headed out the door. His name may be Adam but she wasn't Eve, and this sure as the devil wasn't paradise.

Three

Adam had done many things in his life that were subject to question. Few, however, had left him as baffled as his decision to stay on at Shady Point Lodge. Bent over the deck floor of Cabin Number 8 several mornings after he'd fished one Joanna should-have-been-a-drill-sergeant Taylor out of the drink, he was still trying to sort it all out.

Pounding a nail home, he told himself he'd stayed because he needed the solitude, *not* because of the bossy, brassy redhead who was his temporary straw boss.

He wasn't there because he was running, either. He'd never run from anything in his life. Not from Vietnam, not from a hundred filthy assignments, not from Annie. She'd been the one to run—from him and from their marriage. She'd had good cause on both counts.

This morning, with the air still nippy and sharp and with a clean scent he'd never known before, their disastrous marriage and his life in Detroit seemed a lifetime away.

He lined up another board and flashed on a memory that was not so distant: Frank lying dead on the cold liquor-store floor. He forced the picture away only to find it replaced with another: The boy, his eyes wild with surprise and pain, his hand clutched over his own chest as if trying to staunch the flow of blood from Adam's bullet.

Despite the morning chill, a bead of sweat trickled down his temple. He wiped it away with an unsteady hand and told himself again that he was *not* running.

He was just running down, he admitted wearily. Claypool had been right. He sat back and stared out over the lake, remembering the conversation with his sergeant the day he'd left Detroit . . .

. . . The rattle of loose glass in Sergeant Claypool's Fifth Precinct office door had announced his arrival.

"You're late," Jack Claypool said without looking up from the report on his desk.

Sensing his boss's tension, Adam limped to the chair opposite the desk and dropped into it. "Those damn things are going to kill you," he warned, referring to the cigarette that perpetually dangled from the corner of Jack's mouth.

Jack drew deeply on his cigarette. "Occupational hazard. But then I guess I don't need to talk to you about hazards, do I? How is the leg anyway?"

"Fine. The leg's fine."

Silence settled over them like the hazy layers of drifting smoke as Adam waited for Jack to get past the small talk and on to the reason he'd called him in.

Outside the tiny cubicle the Detroit PD laughingly referred to as Claypool's office, the phones rang incessantly, victims cried, and suspects protested at being booked. On the city streets five stories below, the serrated howl of a response car siren faded to a low, hollow moan.

Impatient with the wait, Adam leaned forward in

his chair. "We going to sit here and play patty cake all morning, or did you call me in here for a reason?"

Jack ground out his cigarette among the butts in an overflowing ashtray. "You're one of the best vice cops under my command, Adam . . . but you're also my friend. And as your friend, I've got to know. When are you going to let it go?"

So that was the way the wind blew, Adam thought wearily as Jack went on.

"In all my years on the force, I've had luck on my side. I've never lost a partner, but I can relate to what you're going through. You and Frank were together fifteen years. That's no short reel."

"You've sung this hymn before, Jack," he said, closing his eyes and slumping back in the chair.

"Well, stick around, buddy, you've only heard the first verse. Man, I'm desperate to reach you. One way or another this hair shirt of yours has got to come off. Frank was a good man. A good cop. Mourn him. Miss him. But for God's sake, don't allow his death to be your own undoing. It was not your fault. And think about it, Adam. It could have been you. If you'd taken that bullet somewhere other than in your thigh, we would have buried you along with Frank. His number was up and there was nothing you could have done about it. As for the boy, he was destined to come to that kind of end. If it hadn't been you, it would have been some other cop or some hood that got him."

Adam worked his jaw and stared at the cracked tile on the floor.

"Deaf ears," Jack muttered as he fished around in his hip pocket for a roll of antacids. He popped one into his mouth, then went on. "Everything I say to you falls on deaf ears. Dammit, Adam! It's been almost two months. You've got to let the guilt go. It's not yours to bear."

He pushed himself upright. "Look—I'm fine.

Save your hellfire and brimstone for some rookie who needs a pep talk. Just give me an assignment. I'm ready to go back on the street."

"Like hell. Look at you. You don't sleep. You obviously don't eat. Your hands are shaking so bad, you'd blow a hole through your own gut before you ever unholstered your gun. You weren't responsible for Frank's death, but I'd sure as hell be responsible for what happened to your new partner if I saddled him with you in this condition."

"Send me out alone then. I need to work."

"You are working."

"Pushing paper and filling in on dispatch is not what I do."

"You won't even be doing that much longer if you don't get your act together. I can't protect you forever. The big boys are watching. Soon they'll quit asking for my opinion. They're talking about disability leave, Adam. A permanent leave."

"My leg is fine," he said succinctly.

"Your leg is not fine, but even if it were, your leg is not the problem. They want to know if I think Dursky, the supercop, has been pushed beyond the breaking point. If I've got a loose cannon on my hands."

For the first time since entering the office, he met Jack's gaze and held it.

"You're balancing on a very thin edge here, Adam. I can't let you on the street this way and you know it. Level with me," he commanded after a ringing silence. "Are you on the booze again?"

It was a fair question. He couldn't even be angry that Jack had asked it. "No. No booze."

Jack reached into his breast pocket for another cigarette. "How long you been dry? Has it been ten years yet?"

"Eleven, give or take a month." Give or take exactly one month and twenty-two days, he added silently.

"Booze was my answer for a time there too," Jack said quietly.

"You can save the Pollyanna rhetoric, Jack. We're both big boys and we both know how to handle our own problems."

"I'm glad you feel that way, because right now you're my biggest problem and I've decided on a way to solve it." Jack drew deeply on his cigarette. "I'm extending your leave. Starting today, you've got another month off. Adam—I've got no choice and in my opinion, neither do you."

He could feel what color was left in his face drain like blood from a reopened wound. The tension, bowstring tight in its intensity, was manageable only because of the feelings he and Jack held for each other.

"If you take my job, you take everything."

"I'm trying to save your job. If you were thinking rationally, you'd realize that fact." Jack hesitated, then leveled the final blow. "I'll need the badge, Adam. And the gun. . . ."

That had been four days ago and even now, Adam broke out in a cold sweat just thinking about it. He'd been numb as he'd dug into his hip pocket, drawn out his wallet, and flipped it open.

He remembered staring at his badge, polishing the worn insignia with a long, thoughtful stroke of his thumb. Twenty years he'd carried the Detroit PD badge. It should have been harder to give up. In the end, it hadn't been hard enough. He'd suddenly realized Jack was right, and that he was tired of fighting.

Without another word, he'd unfastened his shoulder holster and laid both it and the badge on Jack's desk. Then he'd left the precinct, retreating to his empty apartment. Not for the first time since

Frank's death, he'd considered drinking himself into blissful, mind-numbing oblivion.

He hadn't. Instead, he'd packed a duffel and checked in on John. Assured that his condition was stable, he'd caught a bus out of town. Almost twenty-four hours later, he'd walked down a rocky path toward a run-down resort, the most beautiful lake he had ever seen, and a redheaded woman/child with defiant green eyes.

Bottom line: Jack was right. He *did* need the rest. The lake and the North country had struck a chord in him. Here he could fill up on clean and quiet and simple. He needed this break from the stench and the noise of the city, and from the adrenaline rushes that came with his job.

His job. It unsettled him that he didn't miss it.

John Taylor's kid, however, unsettled him even more.

He looked up as she walked by and noticed again what he'd been trying not to notice since he'd decided to stay. There was less child and more woman to her than he was able to ignore.

She was wearing her standard uniform of jeans, T-shirt, and a carpenter's apron slung around her ridiculously boyish hips. She'd tied a faded blue bandanna around her forehead to hold back that riotous tangle of hair, and for the life of him, all he wanted to do at that moment was touch it. He wanted to see if it was as silky as it looked, if it would lay heavy in his callused hands.

She played the part of a prickly cactus with an amazing amount of panache, yet he sensed that hidden beneath the needles was a caring, giving woman. A woman a man could get lost in, then found in, emerging strong and whole again in the process.

Lord, where had that come from? he asked himself, tearing his gaze from her and slamming another nail home. He'd like to believe he reacted to her only because she was John's kid, or because he hadn't been able to ignore the fact that she was struggling.

Since when have you ever wanted to play the role of father/protector? he asked himself as he set the final nail. Maybe since he'd found her drowning with that damn duck in her arms. The thought of what could have happened to her if he hadn't been there prompted a wrenching in his gut reminiscent of the hit he'd taken in Nam.

He shook it off. He'd never been anyone's father, and wet-nursing a brat in red braids didn't meet his definition of fun.

So he just kept coming back to the only other motive, and it was much too dangerous to entertain. He was damned near old enough to be her father, he told himself. If he was so hot to get laid, he should have taken care of it before he left the city.

He renewed the promise he'd made when he'd decided to stay. She was off-limits. Period. He had nothing to offer her but short-term. Though she'd fight the notion to the bitter end, the little spitfire had commitment written all over her. He had no intention of committing to anything. She might be a brat, but she deserved a damn sight better than a one-night stand with the likes of him.

Even if it killed him, he wasn't going to lay a hand on her. Not even, he vowed, stealing a last lingering look at her trim little butt as she walked away, a finger.

It was one of those days that if she could have found a way, Jo would have bottled and saved it, so she could retrieve it later to savor and enjoy. The lake was pastel blue and portrait-still, a mirror of the sky that held court to a brilliantly burning sun. The air was warm and fragrant with scents of the approaching fall. The man at her side was, for a change, quite mellow, his usual scowl replaced by a thoughtful, if disconcerting, stare.

She'd set out a noon lunch of sandwiches, peanut butter cookies, and chips at one of the picnic tables overlooking the lake. Cooper lounged in the grass at the head of the table, conspicuously alert for handouts.

If anyone had come upon the scene they would think they'd stumbled on the epitome of serene domestic bliss. A woman, her man, and a dog. She'd have laughed at the notion if it hadn't suddenly seemed so appealing.

Her man. Propping her elbows on the picnic table, she dug into her sandwich and told herself to snap to. Since when had she started painting herself into pictures that reeked of romance and happily ever after? Since Adam Dursky had limped onto the scene, that's when.

Losing her appetite, she set her sandwich back on the table. Maybe once, long ago, she'd wanted that scenario. Forcing herself to remember what had happened the last time she'd thought she had a man pegged, she put on the skids. She'd believed she'd seen something in that other man that hadn't been there. Integrity for one thing, love for another. All she'd gotten for her efforts was heartache.

She was wise enough now to know she could do just fine without a man . . . especially a man like Adam.

He'd leave here the way he came—a stranger.

She would miss him, though, she admitted as she indulged in a long, assessing look at his profile. She'd miss the mystery and the man.

His face was a study in symmetry. His nose was Spartanly straight and perfectly positioned beneath that surly, brooding brow. The sunlight shining on his angular features did nothing to diminish his rugged appeal. Instead, it added depth and character, and emphasized that undeniable vulnerability held in check by inner strength. And it drove home the fact that although the shaded hollows below his cheekbones could have been etched from bronze, and his jaw chiseled from granite, he was cast from anything but stone. He was flesh and blood and substance.

She tried not to think of him in those terms, as a man who felt pain and regret. Yet it was becoming increasingly harder to convince herself that he was the hard, cynical rebel he'd like her to believe he was.

The way the light played across his face made him look younger than she'd originally guessed. Late thirties, maybe early forties. As she'd already discovered, he had the body of a young man. He was hard and lean, and his skin, stretched taut over all that sinew and muscle, had drunk color from the sun the past few days, giving him a natural, honeyed tan. Her gaze dropped to his leg and she wondered again how he'd come by that limp.

When she looked up again, it was to see he'd caught her watching him. The unrest in his eyes set her pulse skittering. After several thick, damning seconds, he turned away. Several more seconds passed before she realized he'd asked her a question.

"I'm sorry, what did you say?"

"I asked you if you really think you've got a prayer of making this place pay?"

So, she thought, working hard to contain a grin. The cynic speaks. Leave it to him to draw up whatever barrier had been in danger of being breached between them.

He was really very predictable. In some small way, she found that assuring, even mildly amusing. He didn't want to deal with whatever was happening between them any more than she did. For that she thanked him silently and answered his question as a reward.

"Well, I'll tell you," she began conversationally. "Just as soon as word gets out that Shady Point is back in business and better than ever, old customers and new ones will be calling in with bookings. What?" she asked, unable to suppress a smile at his doubtful look. "You don't see the possibilities?"

He grunted, swallowing a mouthful of sandwich. "I see possibilities all right. They all start and end with bankruptcy."

"Exactly." She nibbled on a chip. Shady Point was her favorite subject, and she was glad to share her strategy with him. "That's how I got the lodge back."

His scowl deepened. "Bankruptcy?"

"Yup." Relaxing a little, she dangled her pop can between her fingers and caught his eye.

He looked quickly away, frowning at a new blister forming on his palm. She could see that he was interested, and decided, just for the fun of it, to wait until he made the next move.

The wait paid off with classic Dursky sarcasm. "Am I going to be privileged enough to be enlightened with a more detailed explanation, or is this where your little economics lesson ends?"

She took a sip of her pop, enjoying both his dry wit and his curiosity. "I wouldn't have thought economics would be a topic that would interest a man like you, Dursky."

"A man like me," he mused aloud, as if wondering what kind of man she'd decided she was dealing with. She saw it again, that spark in his eyes that hinted at a sense of humor. Fascinated, she waited to see what came next. What came next was that he baited her.

"Well, I'll tell you, little girl . . ."

She automatically shot him a cautioning glare, and he grinned. An honest-to-goodness, no-holds-barred, thoroughly engaging grin. She was enthralled.

"Sorry," he said, not sounding sorry at all. "I'll tell you, *boss*, it really *doesn't* interest me. I'm just trying to figure out if you add with the same set of numbers as the rest of us."

Feeling easier with him than she ever had, she decided to entertain his curiosity. "Bankruptcy was to my benefit," she explained, "because the bank just kept passing my father's bad paper from one new owner to another, and each only succeeded in taking the place from bad to worse. This spring I convinced the loan officer that I'd have a better chance than the others at paying off the note because I'm a native and I know Shady Point. I know what it needs to make it profitable again."

"What it needs," he mumbled, "is a bulldozer."

"Shows how much you know. You see, if I can get the place prettied up by the end of the month, the bank is going to be a lot more willing to hand me the additional loan I need to buy the land when it goes up for auction the first of November."

He took a huge bite of a cookie and tossed the rest to Cooper. "Auction?"

"Auction. The first of November."

"I got that part, Red. But you're talking in circles. Why is property that you're already buying going up for auction?"

"It's a little complicated."

"Try me."

"Okay, but pay attention. What I'm *buying* from the bank are the buildings. What's going up for *auction* is the land they're built on. Lake Kabetogama is circumferenced by a state park. In addition, the state owns all the lakeshore lots and currently holds leases with the resort owners and the private home owners scattered along the shoreline."

He frowned absently as Cooper ambled over and begged for more cookies, slapping a paw on his thigh. "So you own the buildings but not the land they're built on. Doesn't sound like too stable a business proposition."

"It isn't. That's why it's about to change. The state, responding to lobbying from the leaseholders, has decided to sell—"

"At auction the first of November," he concluded, as comprehension dawned. "But why the auction? Why doesn't the state just offer the land to the leaseholders at a fair market price?"

"That was the original intent when this whole business started. But it got sticky when they turned up a law that requires all state-owned lands to be sold at public auction."

"So what you're telling me," he said after feeding Cooper another cookie and thinking it through, "is that you could put all this time and money into the place, then someone could outbid you and buy it out from under you?"

She shrugged, trying to appear unconcerned. "Conceivably, yes, that could happen. But look around you, Dursky. Who in their right mind would want to buy this place?"

"You've got a point there," he said, but he was still frowning.

"Give me a little credit here. There's a reason I've been back since spring and haven't started fixing things up until this month. The state held an open house on the property the end of August as the first phase of the auction process. Everyone who ever thought they wanted to own a fishing resort showed up. They all saw what you see and most of them went away shaking their heads."

"I take it the auction isn't held on the property?"

"Bingo. By November first, Shady Point will be

reduced to a number on a program in the auction hall, and anyone who came to the open house in August will cringe and figure the state will be lucky to give it away. I'll be the one and only bidder."

Cooper woofed impatiently. Adam threw him another cookie. "One thing bothers me."

"Only one?" she asked, taking her cue from his sarcasm as she snagged the cookies and set them out of his reach.

"It seems to me you're pinning a lot of hope on a flawed theory. What if one of those prospective buyers had the foresight to look past the run-down buildings and recognized the value of the lake frontage? If they outbid you, what happens?"

Her optimism gave way to a blank stare. He'd pointed out her biggest fear with cutting clarity. It wasn't anything she didn't already know or worry about, but it was something she didn't like to face. "Then I'll be forced to sell the buildings to the buyer for the state's appraised value. But that's not going to happen."

It *couldn't* happen, she assured herself. Still, the threat hung heavy in the air, and the easy mood was broken. She could see by his dark look that he thought she was crazy. Well, she was crazy to ever have thought she could confide in him, or that he'd ever give a rat's rear end about her or Shady Point.

Rising swiftly, she stuffed the remains of their lunch into the picnic basket. "And this work isn't going to get finished if we sit here and jaw all day."

The little fool, Adam thought as he watched her walk up the hill to the main lodge, Cooper bounding at her heels. She'd do just as well to pin her hopes on a wave and expect it to stay put.

He was glad he wasn't going to be around to

watch her dream turn into a nightmare. Damn glad that come the first of November, he'd be gone and what happened to Jo Taylor and Shady Point Lodge would not be his problem.

Scrubbing a palm over his jaw, he looked at the lush forest surrounding him, at the cabins that were beginning to look more rustic than ruined, at the lake that had as many moods as a restless lover. And he thought of the woman who would be devastated if she lost it all.

He didn't sleep much that night for thinking about her and her damn stubborn innocence. And her eyes. And that hair. As he lay awake he fought to purge from his mind the image he'd carried since he'd dragged her and that damn duck half-drowned and sputtering from the lake.

Her wet white T-shirt had been nearly transparent, and her nipples, puckered like raisins beneath it, were berry-brown against the roundness of her small, exquisite breasts. Her hair, sodden heavy ringlets of amber fire, had framed her pixie face, a face that for all its innocence, was the face of a woman.

But what singed and burned and tugged at the edge of his consciousness was the sight of a leather knife sheath strapped high and tight on the inside of her leg. The leather had imprinted itself into her surprisingly supple flesh, and that night, like every previous night, he fell asleep wondering how that suppleness would respond to his questing mouth, how his body would fit between the cradle of her thighs.

The memory of her was still tugging at him as they worked in silence for the better part of an hour the next morning. He was still fighting the pull when she shot him a nervous sideways glance. "How do you know my father?"

He looked over at her, glad for the diversion and surprised she'd finally broached the subject.

It was about time, he told himself gruffly. Until yesterday she'd studiously avoided any conversation other than what related to the work in progress on the cabins. That she was curious about John wasn't an issue; it was whether or not that curiosity was ever going to get the best of her.

Now that it had, he weighed out his answer. He wasn't sure how much she was ready to hear . . . or how much he wanted to tell.

"AA," he said finally, deciding to lay it out in a straight line. When she didn't react, he elaborated. "Alcoholics Anonymous."

"I know what it is," she snapped, and hopped off the deck like she'd snagged a sliver in her bottom.

"Then you know what it means," he said tightly.

She looked at him long and hard and, he decided, with decidedly too much disappointment. "It means you're just like him."

He smiled grimly. "I'm not dying, if that's what you had in mind."

He'd said it more harshly than he'd intended. The bruised look in her eyes told him how deeply he'd cut. Hardening himself to her wounded gaze, he went on. "But if you meant, am I an alcoholic? Yeah, I am."

She studied him for a long, searching moment before turning toward the main lodge, snapping orders over her shoulder as she went. "If you're done here, finish patching the roof on Number Three, then go ahead and put up the new eaves."

"Anything you say, boss lady," he said, glaring at her departing back.

She thought she was so damn tough, he mused. Well, just once he'd like to see her react by showing her feelings instead of running away from them when they got too hot to handle.

When he asked himself why he wanted to know how she felt—particularly about his problem—he didn't like the answer. It was because he *cared* what she thought of him, dammit. That realization rubbed like the hammer handle against his new blister.

Another two days passed before she broke ground again. He caught her trying to lug a flat of shingles up a ladder by herself. When he called her on it, she rounded on him.

"I don't need you or any other man telling me how to run my business, Dursky. You *take* orders here, not *give* them."

He saluted smartly and told her by all means, to have at it. She did, practically breaking her scrawny neck in the process.

That night she apologized. He wasn't sure which one of them was more surprised.

"Look," she began uneasily over a supper of fried chicken and potatoes, "I shouldn't have jumped on you like that this afternoon. I know you were trying to help."

He buttered his bread and shrugged. "No problem."

"It's just that I'm not used to anyone . . ."

"Helping?" he prompted when she seemed at a loss.

She nodded, looking sheepish.

"I noticed."

He continued eating in silence. She did little more than push her food around on her plate with her fork.

"Is it . . . the drinking? I mean . . . is it still a problem for you?" she asked finally.

Surprised that she wanted to know, he met her eyes across the table. He read her look for what it was. She wanted him to say no, it wasn't a problem.

He wanted to tell her it wasn't. Beyond that, he wanted to tell her she shouldn't be wondering, that she could get in big trouble by even caring. So he made sure she knew the truth, because he knew she wouldn't like it.

Bracing his forearms on the edge of the table, he leaned toward her. "It'll always be a problem, Red. But if you're asking me if I have a habit of falling off the wagon, the answer is no. At least not lately. But then, nothing's a given. You could drive me to it yet."

It was a stupid thing to say. He should have known she'd take him seriously. She put down her fork and stared at her lap.

"When I was younger," she said softly, "I always wondered if that's what happened with my father. If it was me, not my mother's death, that made him drink."

You still wonder, don't you, Red? he mused, damning himself for his insensitivity. Not wanting to be affected by her pain but accepting that he was, he sighed and slouched back in his chair.

"Alcoholism is an illness, Jo. When your father wandered into Detroit a few years ago and into that first AA meeting, he was as down as a man can get. I'd been there, where he was, and I knew what he was going through. I suppose that's why we connected."

She shoved her chair back from the table and began clearing away their dirty dishes.

"He's been dry for over a year now," he added, deciding not to let her run away this time.

Facing the sink, she put her head down and gripped the counter. He could feel her tension, almost taste the effort it took her to hold on to her control.

"One year out of ten," she said. "Too little too late, wouldn't you say? Look what it's done to him."

And look what it's done to you, he added silently. He pushed away from the table, the scrape of his chair against the oak floor shattering the silence. He carried his dishes to the sink. Leaning a hip against the counter, he crossed his arms over his chest and looked down at her. She was so small standing there beside him. Small and hurting. It was suddenly too much to ask of himself not to reach out to her.

"Jo," he said, touching a hand to her cheek. She was trembling. For that matter, so was he. He gripped her slim shoulders and gently turned her toward him. "With an alcoholic there are never any guarantees. But John's on top of his problem now. If this complication with his heart hadn't flared up—"

"No guarantees?" she cut in. Her tone was bitter, but her eyes were filled with a wild desperation. "Well, I'm sorry but I *need* guarantees—and don't think I don't know what you're trying to do. You're trying to get me to admit that I miss him and to make me realize I need him back here. Well, let me tell you what it's going to take to make that happen."

She tried to pull away. He wouldn't let her. So she issued her ultimatum, her green eyes flashing like cut glass.

"You *guarantee* me that if my father comes out of this alive he'll be the man I knew before he turned to alcohol as an antidote for his pain. You *guarantee* me he'll never drink again and I'll welcome him back. Otherwise, you can forget it. I won't watch him turn into someone I neither know nor like. I won't watch him die like that. Not again. Not ever again."

Her voice was shaking, her eyes suspiciously bright, and like the first time he saw her, he thought of the child within.

"How old are you, Red?" he asked softly, not expecting an answer. "Old enough to know that fairy tales have no basis in fact, I'd guess." He paused and watched her thick lashes flutter down to shadow her cheeks. "Old enough to know that real life doesn't come with guarantees," he continued in the same even tone. "Just promises that even with the best of intentions sometimes get broken."

Defiance laced with pride hardened the eyes that met his. "What I'm old enough to know is that the only thing in life I can count on is myself. What?" she asked with a defensive lift of her chin when he was silent. "Don't you want to argue with me on that count? Don't you want to tell me that he can make it because *you* made it? That you're living proof the odds can be beaten? That there are people in this world I can count on and you're one of them?"

Though she was pushing for a denial, she couldn't camouflage the hope in her eyes. He also saw something else. Mixed with the defensiveness and the pain, he recognized the way she was looking at him—the way she had *been* looking at him more and more often lately. It was the look a woman gave a man when there was more than business on her mind. That knowledge licked along his senses like a slow burning flame. Her nearness fed the fire.

Fighting the response he wanted to give her, he looked her squarely in the eye. "You never beat the disease, Red," he said, intending to quell her interest then and there. "You just beat it back, and every day you hope you've got a stick big enough to do the job."

"You've managed. You haven't let it ruin your life."

But he had almost let it ruin Annie's, he thought wearily, feeling that old flicker of guilt that always accompanied her memory. While it was never meant to be between them, she'd been the one good thing in his life back then. He thought of her softness and all the other qualities he'd almost destroyed before he'd done the right thing and let her go.

Suddenly, he missed what they'd almost had together. Looking deep into the eyes of this woman who, as unlikely as it seemed, might be able to give him what Annie never could, he felt a keen sense of regret. He had to do the right thing for her, too, and that meant leaving her alone.

But her eyes revealed so much. Asked so much. What they were asking for right now had less to do with guarantees than with need. A need that was mutual and demanding.

Why he'd thought she'd discourage him when she hadn't had sense enough to send him packing that very first day, he'd never know. She didn't have the sense God gave a moth. Look at her. She was flying headlong into a fire, her eyes wide open, her lips parted, as good as asking him to help her get burned.

Suddenly, he just couldn't say no. Not to his own demands or hers. Not to the long, empty years or the sweet honest desire shining in her eyes.

He damned her for tempting him, damned himself for succumbing, then he did the unforgivable. He lowered his head and with a groan of defeat, covered her mouth with his own.

His breath stalled in his chest as he met lips that were petal soft and pliant, breath as hesitant and hushed as a whisper. The innocent response of her mouth set his pulse racing and ignited a fever in his blood that should never have been coaxed to flame.

Losing the token battle with his will, he drew her against him and allowed his hands to roam greedily over the slight, perfect body he'd taken to bed in his mind every night since he'd arrived. He indulged in the reality of holding her at last, relishing each white-hot contact as her small breasts met and molded to his chest, as her hips and belly nestled against the thick ache in his loin.

She was supple and yielding and dangerously needy as she moved against him, whimpering her surprise and her hunger, until the desire prowling the edge of his sanity became a wild, raging beast.

She clung to him. With complete trust and a total lack of fear she opened to him, unwittingly unleashing his long suppressed desire. He pillaged her mouth with his tongue, stole her offering for the treasure that it was, and reveled in the knowledge that she returned his passion full measure.

This was no child in his arms. This was a woman, strong and alive and full of fire. A woman who would never bend against her will to any man. Yet she was bending now, passionately, desperately, as the kiss lengthened and deepened, transcending the bounds of physical need to a realm that was far more dangerous. There were feelings here. Deep feelings that rimmed the dark side of his reason and should never have been allowed into the light.

The thought that saved him from getting lost in her taste and her trembling body was how easy it would be to take her—and how hard it would be later to witness her pain. There would be pain. If he let this go further, when he left her—and he *would* leave her—there would be pain.

Steeped in that knowledge, he roughly set her away from him.

Her eyes were dazed, her breath, like his, labored and shallow.

"You want someone to count on, Red?" he said in a strained, angry whisper. "Well, you just found out that someone isn't me. A strong man wouldn't have kissed you. He'd have kept his promise to himself and left you the hell alone."

Looking confused and achingly vulnerable, she just stared at him. Her wide-eyed trust fueled his anger.

"You shouldn't have let me do that, dammit. And I never should have let it happen." He dropped his hands from her shoulders and backed away. "You want guarantees, little girl? Just so there's no confusion and no disillusion down the road, let me give you one. Don't *ever* count on me for anything. On that front, I *can* give you a guarantee. I'll only let you down."

Four

The best way to deal with Adam Dursky, Jo decided the next morning, was to stay away from him. At the crack of dawn she'd issued concise, clipped orders on the work she wanted him to do that day. Then she'd headed in the opposite direction, telling herself there was nothing the man could offer her but trouble.

Trouble, unfortunately, had never looked more appealing.

The day was still new when she grudgingly admitted that physically distancing herself from him wasn't the answer. While sorting through an assortment of fishing tackle in the boathouse, she kept thinking about what had happened between them the night before. "Don't *ever* count on me for anything," he'd warned her. "I'll only let you down."

She knew he was right. She'd known he wasn't a man to get involved with the day he'd limped into the lodge with his duffel in hand and his attitude riding on his shoulder. Yet as she had when she'd lain alone in her bed all those nights, when she'd work alongside him all those days, she caught herself wondering what it would be like to be important to a man like him, to make a difference to a man like him, to be loved by him.

Upset by her thoughts, she tried to come to terms with the reason he affected her so. Was it because there was so much more to him than he wanted her to see? That despite his cynicism and his claim to the contrary, he was a strong man? A man who kept his confidences and his problems to himself; a man who was hurting and protected that hurt like a dog guarding a bone.

She'd felt that hurt last night, felt the need in him. His kiss had touched her deeply. Though he had fought the feeling, she knew it had touched him too. For a long, aching moment he had held her like she was the one thing in his life worth hanging on to. Then he'd come to his senses and let her go. When she caught her reflection in the window, she was reminded of why.

Staring back at her from the dusty pane were eyes too wide set to be pretty, a complexion too splattered with freckles to be taken seriously, and a nose that shouted pixie, not woman.

Closing her eyes against the harsh reality of the image she presented, she reminded herself that a man like Adam Dursky couldn't afford to waste emotions on someone like her. On a kid, as he was so quick to label her. On a little girl who didn't merit the attention reserved for a mature woman.

She touched a trembling hand to her mouth and remembered his kiss. That kiss had made a lie of his claim that he saw her only as a child. It had been a kiss a man gives a woman. It had tasted of passion and temptation, and the solid heat of his body pressed to hers had delivered an unmistakable message. He had wanted her. Even more, in that moment he had needed her.

But in the next moment, she reminded herself grimly, he had let her go.

She ought to be thankful that he, at least, had

shown some sense. In a bid to ignore the sweet, aching swirls of arousal churning low in her belly, she returned to her work, reminding herself of one other indisputable fact. He had a problem. The same one that had taken away her father. The same one that would eventually take him away too.

The familiar sound of Steve Miller's pickup rumbling down the drive and braking to a stop by the lodge's back door saved her from dealing with the sense of loss she felt over that conclusion.

Knowing that as soon as Steve hopped out of the Park Department's truck he'd be popping into her kitchen and hitting her up for coffee, she poked her head out the boathouse door. "I'm down here. Grab a cup and come on down."

"You want one too?" Steve called before he slipped inside to help himself.

"No thanks. I've had enough."

More caffeine was exactly what she didn't need. Steve, however, was a welcome diversion. She didn't want to think about Adam anymore, about things that could never be between them.

Dropping what she was doing, she walked outside to meet Steve. Her heart executed a quick shuffle when she saw two men heading toward her. Steve, dark-haired and grinning, sauntered down from the lodge with a steaming mug of coffee in his hand. Adam, blond and brooding, limped down from cabin number 10 where he'd been working on the plumbing, a pipe wrench gripped tightly in his hand. Cooper, who had taken to dividing his time between Jo and Adam, trotted happily at Adam's side.

When the two men spotted each other, their steps slowed momentarily. They exchanged curt, silent nods.

"Is this a business or a social call?" she asked

Steve in an attempt to dispel a tension she suddenly sensed but couldn't define.

"Since when do I have to have a reason to stop in and see you?" Steve asked with his usual cocky grin. His tone, however, sounded a wee bit territorial.

Adam's frowning reaction to that tone had her completely baffled. Certain she was only imagining something was amiss, she teased Steve good-naturedly. "Since part of my tax dollar started paying your salary, *Officer* Miller. I don't like to see my public servants loafing on the job."

"I'm just about to go on duty, okay? So save your smart mouth for someone who will appreciate it." Though his remark was purposefully playful, he looked pointedly at Adam.

"Oh, sorry," she said. Instead of introducing the men, she'd been comparing Adam's rangy, rebellious presence to Steve's immaculate conservation officer's uniform and all-American good looks, and wondering why Adam seemed the more attractive of the two. "Steve, this is Adam Dursky. Adam's helping me fix up the place. Adam, this is Steve Miller. Steve's an old friend . . . when he isn't playing Dudley Do-Right to the hilt and giving me a hard time."

Adam wiped a work-soiled hand on his jeans before extending it to Steve. "Miller."

Steve returned the handshake, openly sizing Adam up. Jo leaned back against the boathouse doorframe, too stunned to believe what she was seeing. Steve looked possessive and protective. He was eyeing Adam as if he'd like to escort him out of the state, preferably in handcuffs.

And Adam—incredible as it seemed—looked unapologetically jealous.

The fact that Adam's jealousy was directed at Steve was ridiculous. Steve, was . . . well, just Steve. They'd grown up together, shared the same teething rings, the same secrets, the same pup tent on more than one overnight. He'd never been anything but brother material.

The fact that Adam was jealous at all was just too much to digest. Last night he'd made it glass clear that he wasn't about to let anything happen between them.

So the loner wasn't so sure he wanted to be alone after all, she thought, feeling an unwarranted burst of happiness rush through her. Steeped in that knowledge, she let a totally inappropriate smile develop.

And then, like a wave slamming over the dock during a storm, the truth of her own dilemma drenched her. Her smile gave way to a distressed frown. Adam wasn't the only one in trouble here. For all her carefully orchestrated aloofness, for all her practiced shows of hostility, she'd been quietly, hopelessly, falling in love with Adam Dursky.

"Heard you'd hired someone on," she heard Steve say through a foggy haze of alarm. "Dursky," he repeated. "I don't believe I recognize the name. You from the Falls?"

Adam shook his head. "Detroit."

"Detroit? You're a long way from home."

"Yeah, I guess I am." He turned to Jo. "You got any more wrenches around here?"

"Wr-wrenches?" she stammered, still struggling to come to grips with her discovery. "Yes, sure, wrenches. They're inside. Is there a problem?" Was there a problem? she asked herself, swallowing a panicky laugh. Was the sky blue? Did Paul McCartney sing? Was there a fool born every minute? Oh Lord, what had she gone and done?

Grim-faced and apparently oblivious to her distress, Adam shouldered past her and into the boathouse. "I need a different size for those pipes."

Steve scowled in silence while Adam rummaged

around the shelves and finally came up with the tools he needed. His hands were full when he walked back outside.

"Miller." He nodded again, then he and Cooper headed up the path to the cabin.

Steve turned to Jo, his dark eyes narrowed. "Are you out of your ever-loving mind?"

"Yes," she muttered, more to herself than to Steve. "I believe I am."

Still shaken, she watched Adam leave, wondering if there was a chance he, too, was involved in this more deeply than he realized. Wondering, with a detached sense of concern, if she wanted him to be.

"Who *is* that guy?" Steve asked incredulously. "Where the hell did he come from?"

She forced her attention back to Steve. "Didn't I just hear him tell you all that?"

"Don't get smart with me, Joanna. You know what I mean. And besides that, I don't think I like the way he looks at you."

Her gaze strayed again to Adam—to the broad expanse of his back, the narrow cut of his hips. "How does he look at me?" she asked, wishing she hadn't sounded so breathless.

Steve rubbed a hand across his jaw. "Like he'd like to have you for breakfast, lunch, *and* dinner."

She couldn't stop her grin, an utterly victorious, absolutely uncalled for female grin. Her ship was swiftly sinking and she was blissfully waving oxygen good-bye.

Steve groaned. "You'd better watch it, girl. How could you just up and hire a stranger anyway? Particularly him? For the love of Mike, Jo, he looks like a thug."

Her silence earned her another scowl.

"Did you find out *anything* about him before you hired him?"

She snorted derisively. "Like if he had something he didn't want me to know, he'd tell me about it? That he'd just up and announce, 'Oh, by the way, I thought you'd like to know I'm an escapee from the state pen. Nothing major—assault with a deadly weapon, a little fuss about a murder-one charge' . . ." She shook her head. "Come on, Steve. Lighten up. Adam's okay."

Her attempt at flippancy didn't fool either of them. "She doesn't know a damn thing about him," Steve said to the sky.

But she did know as much as she needed, more than she wanted, and that knowledge felt both uplifting and regrettably heavy in her hands. "He's a friend of my father, all right?" she said. She didn't want to explore her newfound knowledge with herself, let alone with Steve.

"Your father?" Steve repeated. "How did that happen?"

As quickly and concisely as possible, she told him. "And I don't want to talk about it," she added, sensing more questions coming, questions about her father.

Steve evidently read the determination on her face. Knowing how stubborn she could be, he grudgingly obliged her. "Just promise me one thing, okay? Call me. He gives you any trouble, you call me. Got it?"

"Got it. But don't worry. He isn't giving me any trouble."

Adam came around the corner just then, and the look in his eyes made her a liar. That one look caused more trouble than she'd ever be able to get into by herself. Her heart caught, then skipped wildly as with a fiercely protective glance, he walked back into the boathouse to replace the tools.

Everything she was feeling about Adam was wrong. Nothing they could ever have together could be right. But at that moment, she wanted to be alone with him and confront the issue.

She graced Steve with a manufactured smile. "Haven't you got a forest fire to fight or something? Or are you planning to hang around here all day and give me a hard time?"

Out of the corner of her eye, she saw Adam flash a quick, tight grin.

"Actually, I did have some news," Steve said, looking a little uncomfortable. "You're not going to like it."

She was instantly alert to the edge in his tone. "So let's hear it."

He hesitated, then drew a deep breath. "Jack Carlson's been doing a lot of checking down at the DNR on the footage and specifications on your shoreline."

A cold dread charged through her, trampling over her concerns about Adam. Carlson's inquiries could only mean one thing. He was interested in bidding on the lodge at the auction.

"Carlson," she repeated, as her heart knocked heavily against her chest. "That doesn't make any sense. Jack doesn't have the kind of capital or initiative to buy Shady Point." She warmed to her argument as she thought it through. "Besides, he's near retirement. He wouldn't want to buy the lodge. It's too much work for a man his age."

Steve looked grim. "Word has it, he's not looking for himself, but acting as an agent for some development firm out of the Twin Cities."

Her dread turned instantly to fear. It knotted in her stomach like a fist. "What's the name of the firm?"

"I'm not sure. But I think it's Dream . . . something or other."

Recognizing the company, she said softly, "Dreamscape." The blood thundering in her ears drowned out the peaceful sound of the lake lapping on the shore and the heightening breeze rustling through the birches. "They specialize in revitalizing, in renovating small, out-of-the-way spots into exclusive getaway places for CEO types and their families."

"It's just a rumor, Jo," Steve said hopefully.

"Yeah, right." Feeling the fast, sure weight of defeat flood her limbs and her hopes like lead, she sank to the top step and stared vacantly over the lake. Cooper squeezed in beside her as if sensing her tension, and leaned heavily against her.

"Hey," Steve said. "I'm sorry I had to be the one to tell you, but I didn't want you hearing it from someone else."

She crossed her arms over her upraised knees and lowered her head to rest on them.

"You okay?" he asked.

"Yeah." Without looking up, she waved him away. "Go to work. I'm fine."

But she wasn't fine. Her dream to restore Shady Point as her own was as good as gone, dissolved like the mist the sun burned off the lake in the mornings. She wasn't fine at all.

What was more, she couldn't handle it. She had to get away. As soon as Steve drove out, she rose, walked behind the boathouse, and dragged her kayak out from underneath its protective tarp.

Guessing her intent, Adam followed her as she headed for the dock. "Do you deal with everything you can't handle by running away from it?"

Disillusioned, angry with the world at large, she struck out at the closest target. "Butt out, Dursky. This isn't your concern."

He watched her, his weight slung on his good leg, staring down at her as she settled into the kayak. "Joanna, I know you're upset, but this is not the time to run off half-cocked. Did you hear the weather report this morning?"

"I heard it."

"Then you know you've got no business out on the lake right now."

Balancing her weight as the rippling water rocked the little craft against the dock's wooden pilings, she ignored his concerned frown. "I'll be back long before that front moves in tonight. I just need a little space, okay? Just a couple of hours of breathing room."

She flipped her braid over her shoulder and made to push away.

Adam caught the end of her paddle and held her still in the water.

She glared at him. "I mean it, Dursky. I don't need your flak."

"What you *need*, is for someone to paddle some sense into your obstinate little backside, since it's obvious that's what you're thinking with. Use your head, girl!"

"I'm a big *girl*," she countered sarcastically. With a mighty tug, she jerked the paddle from his hand. "And you're *not* my keeper."

"That's not to say you don't need one," he said, frowning at the sky, then at the vast expanse of blue-green water.

She thought she heard him mumble something about brick walls and blockheads, but short of jumping in after her, there was little he could do to stop her.

"Look . . . don't worry about me," she called as she dug in with deep strokes and set out across the bay. "I'll be all right."

Hours later, with night closing in and the lake boiling around her like a witch's caldron, she clung to that thought like a lifeline. "I'll be all right," she repeated again and again, as if saying so could make it true.

But as mistakes went, she knew this one

ranked right up there among her biggest. This one just might get her killed.

The advertising brochures she'd had made up for next season referred to Kabetogama as "a remote and beautiful glacial lake." The churning black water swirling around her kayak right now bore little resemblance to the placid vacation paradise the layout depicted. In the space of a heartbeat, the glass-smooth lake had begun to live up to the name the Indians had given it long ago: Kabetogama, lake of rough waters.

Since she'd grown up on Kabby, she knew its moods. She could read all the signs. She read them that morning, but devastated by Steve's news, she'd ignored them. Another bright move in a string of monumental blunders, she thought as she fought to ride out another swell.

The storm had come up quickly, catching her far out on open water. She'd barely had time to haul her life vest out from under the hull and buckle it when the first swell hit, forcing her to make a decision. Turning back then had been out of the question. She was out too far. Whichever direction she decided to take—inland toward the north shore, or east toward Jug Island and Blue Fin Bay—the distance had seemed insurmountable. She'd considered the wind and opted for Jug. Then she'd put her head down and stroked for her life as all hell broke loose around her.

Another huge wave slammed across her bow, another in a series of hundreds. Or was it thousands? She'd lost count, was past caring. Shifting her weight instinctively, she dug deep with the paddle and somehow set the struggling kayak right again.

Risking a swipe at her face, she brushed a rain-soaked swatch of hair from her eyes so she could see. Ha. See what? There was nothing but black sky and angry water hammering at her from all sides. Nothing but raging, whitecapped swells and vicious wind battering her bow, trying to turn her, to push her backward and away from her destination. She was exhausted. Adrenaline alone wasn't going to pull her through many more waves like that last one.

If she could just make it to Jug.

That thought sustained her. She had to be close. She had to be!

She thought of Adam, of the way he'd looked when she'd left him. Of the things she'd said and of all the things she might never get to say to him, and suddenly in the midst of it all, nothing else mattered. Not the very real possibility that she'd lose the lodge, not the anguish and despair she'd felt over the loss of her father. What mattered was Adam.

"You are not going to die!" she shouted above the storm's roar. "Not here. Not like this. Not alone."

She'd hardly completed that thought when she was hit by another monstrous wall of water and a desperate yearning to be anywhere but on this damn lake!

Tears of frustration slithered down her chilled cheeks, mingling with the downpour and the frigid spray. She fought her terror and the urge to let the storm take her. Panic wouldn't help. Her stubbornness had dumped her into this mess. Now it could damn well drag her out of it.

"Hang on, Jo, dammit!" she demanded, praying the next stroke of the oar would be her last, the next slap against the kayak's fragile hull would be the shore.

And then, without warning, the lake fell out from underneath her. The kayak dropped with a sickening thud into the belly of a swell, cracking hard with the impact.

The jolt stunned her, then she was sucked

under. Clawing her way back up, she broke the surface, spitting water and gasping for air while the night around her exploded with the sound of rock scraping against wood. The kayak lurched forward, then flipped over on its side again.

She hit the water fighting for her life and came up coughing. Intense pain lanced through her body. Pain and relief. She'd hit rock. Solid unsinkable rock. She'd made it!

Scrambling out of the kayak, she sank chest-deep in the murky water before her feet connected with the slippery floor of the lake bed. She broke free of the undertow and stumbled across the rocks toward safety, where she collapsed on the shore. Gasping for breath, barely aware of the sting of wet sand and sharp stones scraping her face and bare legs, she clung to the island like a lost child reunited with its mother.

The wind screamed. The rain pummeled. But it was the pain that kept her conscious . . . and the chill. It had crept into her blood through ice-cold limbs and settled deep. She lay there shivering until self-preservation instincts urged her to her knees. She knew she had to find shelter, before shock set in.

Shaking with fatigue and cold, she struggled to her feet, shrugged out of the life vest, and beached the kayak more securely. When the storm cleared, she would need it to get back home. At this moment she wasn't taking any bets on when that would be.

Leaning heavily against a peeling birch tree, she caught her breath and squinted into the blackness to get her bearings. She knew Jug well in the daylight. As a child, she'd spent many happy summer hours visiting the island. It had been her special, secret place and was nearly as familiar to her as the area around her north shore lodge. But in pitch-black night and punishing rain, the island was uncharted ground.

Finally, she decided on a route and chanced it. She hiked for what seemed like an hour. Realistically, she knew it couldn't have been more than minutes. Jug was a relatively small island, but she could have easily taken the wrong path. In the dark, one rock looked like another, each stand of trees like the last. Disheartened, she was about to retrace her steps when the pale silhouette of the cabin took shape.

"Thank you," she whispered heavenward, and heaved a shivering sigh of relief.

Weathered by time and the elements, the faded white structure, its pine steps sagging and gray-shingled roof dotted with moss, beckoned like an old friend.

Propelled by the prospect of the dry interior, she quickened her pace. Impatience and exhaustion made her careless. She stumbled over a rock and went down, hard. She cried out as swift, explicit pain shot through her right hand.

Curling into a ball, she clamped her hand to her breast, biting back a wave of nausea. She didn't need to see to know she'd broken it.

Hot tears burned her eyes. "Stupid, stupid, stupid!" she railed, giving in to the anger but not the pain.

That same anger forced her to her feet. Brushing wet leaves and twigs from her face and tangled hair, she started out again. Shivering violently but employing infinitely more care this time, she maneuvered the slippery path to the cabin. Her joints were stiff with cold and her palm already blessedly numb as she reached the rickety porch steps.

She climbed to the top step and swayed heavily against the railing. Too miserable to focus on anything but escaping the cold, she turned the doorknob, put her shoulder to the door, and fell inside.

He was a cop. He'd survived a war. He'd killed men . . . reluctantly, dutifully. Through it all he'd never laid a hand on a woman in anger. Yet tonight, as he fought the lake and the storm, Adam swore to God that if he didn't drown out there, and if he found that little redheaded whelp in one piece, he was going to derive intense personal satisfaction in tearing her apart limb by freckled limb!

Then he was going to pick up the pieces, gather her close, and give thanks to the powers that be that she was alive.

If she was alive.

She will be, he told himself, as if challenging the other possibility would negate it. She had to be alive.

He hated feeling this helpless. He hated this leaky boat and its short-cycling motor. The icy rain and darkness hampering his vision added to his frustration. His ignorance of the lake compounded the fear that he wouldn't find her. There were dozens of islands, miles of shoreline where she could have sought shelter. He had set a course for only one, Jug Island.

He'd pinned all his hopes on a brief conversation they'd had one night, when sounding a little wistful, she'd told him about the cabin on Jug Island. Before she'd caught herself, she'd let it slip that when she was a child, Jug had been a haven of sorts whenever she'd felt threatened.

She'd definitely felt threatened today. That was why she'd run. Her promised two hours had come and gone, then the storm had shown up. She hadn't. He hadn't been able to stay at the lodge and do nothing any longer. He'd gassed up one of her leaky tubs and thrown everything he could think of—food, dry clothes, first-aid supplies, a sleeping bag—into a waterproof duffel. After snagging the map of the lake from the boathouse wall, he'd ignored the swells hammering up over the dock and headed for Jug.

It was a damn fine time to find out he hated the water!

Rain or lake water, he could no longer tell which, beat against his raincoat and slapped him in the face as the small motorboat chopped with agonizing slowness through the pounding swells. More than once, when he was swallowed by the gaping jaws of a wave, he was certain it would be *his* body that someone would find washed up on a remote shore come morning.

Fear for Joanna urged him on. On to where, he was no longer certain. It had been an hour since he'd seen anything but black. He'd long ago lost his sense of direction.

Swearing into the wind, he looked around, and for a brief, teasing moment a window opened up ahead of him. In that elusive instant he caught the outline of a tree-studded shoreline. Gunning the complaining motor, he made a mad dash toward the spot, taking advantage of the only break he'd gotten since night had descended.

The boat lurched forward for several long, frustrating minutes. He was beginning to think he'd missed his mark when he hit land with a serrated screech of wood against rock. The boat plowed recklessly onto the shore, then skidded to an abrupt stop, throwing him headlong over the bow.

He lay flat on his back, trying to catch his breath as the bed of rocks bit into his back and the icy rain pelted his face and slithered down his neck. Rolling onto all fours, he shook his head to clear it and came nose-to-nose with the one thing that could still his thundering heart and ease the burning ache in his thigh—a bright red kayak beached in the underbrush.

He'd found her.

Relief, when it swamped him, was too strong, too consuming. He closed his eyes and willed anger to take its place.

She was going to pay royally for what she'd put him through. The rough water, the wet and cold, the danger to his own life that her stupid, fly-off-the-handle nonsense had placed him in.

And she was going to pay for making him care, damn her. For reducing him to the most vulnerable of creatures—a man with a weakness for one woman.

He rose stiffly to his feet, rummaged around in the shattered remains of the boat, and snagged the duffel. Grim-faced, he slung it over his shoulder and headed inland.

It wasn't long before he spotted the cabin. His head down against the unrelenting downpour, he limped up the rickety steps. Driven by his anger, he shoved open the door and stepped inside.

The cabin was black as a cave, the silence within so wary, he physically felt her fear.

"Joanna?" he called as the wind whipped his raincoat around his legs and slammed the door against the wall.

More silence, then a small, disbelieving whisper. "Adam?"

He heard the rustle of wet clothes in the darkness and her whimper of relief when she fully embraced the truth that it was him.

"Adam." She materialized out of nowhere and launched herself into his arms. The blow knocked him off balance. He staggered back against the wall as she locked her arms around his neck and burrowed against him.

Wrapping his own arms around her instinctively, protectively, he let go of his need to chew a strip of hide off her slim little backside. Anger, for the moment, had to be content to stalk the outskirts of his emotions. A profound, penetrating relief held it at bay. She was here. She was safe.

Without releasing her, he wrestled the door closed, shutting out the driving rain. "Are you okay?" he asked gruffly as he collapsed against the cabin wall again.

Trembling, she tightened her hold and nodded against his chest.

Drowning in the feel of her, in the reality that he had her wrapped securely in his arms, he closed his eyes and lowered his mouth to her hair. "I ought to beat you within an inch of your life."

A beating was the last thing he wanted to give her, though. Instead, he skated his hand upward from her waist, checking for injuries. What he discovered was a delicate framework of ribs that rose and fell with each unsteady breath she drew. What he felt was a heart that fluttered wildly beneath the heel of his hand.

His heart did a dance of its own. "Damn you, Joanna," he growled as he cupped her jaw in his hand and tipped her face to his. Raking the wet tangle of hair back from her face, he searched her eyes in the darkness. They were fire-bright and glistening, not with pain but with longing. He cursed her again. Then he lowered his head and took her mouth in a desperate kiss.

He poured into that kiss all the fear, all the passion, and the barely leashed anger that had brought him to this point. Shifting their bodies until it was her back against the wall, he pressed his weight into hers. His mouth demanded. His hands possessed as she moved against him and moaned into his mouth, not only yielding to his urgency but returning it with stunning demands of her own.

He skimmed his hand down her throat and

chest, never hesitating before closing over her small but distinctly feminine breast. She was so tiny . . . and so needy as she murmured something unintelligible and arched into his hand. She was liquid fire, combustible heat. Her little furnace of a body burned through her wet clothes as her small, responsive nipple tightened against his palm.

He groaned and deepened the kiss with a savage hunger, losing himself somewhere between reason and rage.

It was her yielding, her total trust and acquiescence that finally set him on the right path. Reason somehow intervened, warning him that in the state he was in, if he didn't back away now, he'd take her there, against the wall. No matter how much her murmurs told him she wanted him, he couldn't do that to her.

Breathing hard, he pushed himself away. Anger was his only combatant against the look in her eyes. And his anger, finally, was going to have its say.

Shivering in the absence of Adam's body heat, Jo huddled into herself and listened to his movements in the darkness.

Glass scraped against metal. A match struck flint then burst into flame. The acrid odor of sulfur and kerosene blended with the scent of her own anxiety as he touched fire to wick. The lamp on the table in the middle of the room flared to life. Its blue-yellow flame cast the cabin in diffused light . . . and Adam in harsh, flickering shadows.

A moment ago he'd been protective, steely strength pressed against her. He'd been wild, reckless desire. But the tension in his stance now was as naked as the anger on his face. A new brand of chill shivered up her spine as he replaced the chimney on the lamp and turned to her, impaling her with slate-gray eyes as stony as the profile she'd just assessed.

Not knowing what to make of the change in him, she swallowed thickly, then jumped when he grabbed the duffel from the floor and tossed it at her feet.

"I brought dry clothes." Sounding as caring as a prison guard, he barked his orders. "Get out of those wet ones and put them on."

Cold, hurt, and confused, she just stood there trying to sort through her own feelings so she could identify and deal with his.

He crossed his arms over his chest and regarded her as if she were a child in need of a good lecture—until his gaze dropped to her clingy wet T-shirt. It lingered there with the same heated intimacy as if he'd touched her.

"Adam—"

The look in his eyes stopped her as he forcibly wrenched his attention back to her face. "Out of the clothes, little girl." His gravelly rasp sent her heart skittering. "After that little joyride, I don't have it left in me to wet-nurse a brat who doesn't know enough to come in out of the rain."

Weary of the mixed signals he was sending her, she met his eyes with defiance. "You don't have to wet-nurse anyone. I've told you before, I can take care of myself."

"Why is it then, that every time I turn around I find you in way over your head? No," he growled before she could utter a protest. "I don't want to hear it. None of it." Rage, harsh and cutting, tempered his tone. "Just get out of those clothes. Now. And don't worry." The smile that touched his lips was forced and mocking. "Your virtue's safe with me. My tastes still run more toward women."

With a disdainful look, he turned toward the fireplace, dismissing her.

After the way he'd kissed her, she wasn't about to be dismissed. "And next you're going to tell me that wasn't a *woman* you had backed up against the wall a minute ago."

A slight tightening of his shoulders was the only response he gave her. It wasn't enough. "Or," she went on, "do you have another explanation for what just happened between us?"

He turned to face her. Their gazes tangled and held as the flame in the oil lamp sputtered and flared from orange to white as remnants of a wind gust found its way into the cabin through a crack in the warped pine siding.

"Adrenaline," he stated with a conviction that dared her to dispute it. "Adrenaline is what happened between us. Don't mistake it for anything else."

It was one shove too many in a day marred by disaster. She was cold, shaking, and the pain in her hand had shot past annoying and was working toward agony. She was weary, too, of his Ping-Pong reactions. "You're the one making the mistake, Dursky." Then, using the most vulgar obscenity she knew, she told him what he could do with his adrenaline.

Her pithy suggestion stopped him cold. He cocked a blond eyebrow. "You're right about one thing. No little girl I know uses *that* word."

"For the last time, I am *not* a little girl! And you, more than anyone, know it." Tears of frustration stung her eyes.

"What I know," he began, emphasizing each word, "is that I'm cold and tired . . . mostly tired of putting up with your sass. And before that stubborn chin of yours lifts any higher, I'd suggest you think twice before you take any more chances, especially with me. I'm really not in the mood, so don't push it, Red. I'm about that far from turning you over my knee and peppering your backside with the flat of my hand."

He snatched the duffel, ripped it open, and shook the contents onto the cabin floor. "Now if you aren't out of those wet clothes and into some dry ones by the time I finish building the fire, so help me, I'll strip you myself."

She caught herself short of taunting him to do just that as he shed his wet rain gear and turned back to the fireplace. Instead, she watched him crouch before the hearth and shove kindling onto the grate.

Quietly, pridefully, she made her point. "I *am* a woman, Adam. As soon as you accept that and the fact that you want me as one, maybe we'll both get a little peace of mind."

"A woman wouldn't have run off today." His voice had grown dangerously soft. She thought of cool, smooth silk and sharp-edged steel. "She would have faced the problem and dealt with it. And I'll have peace of mind, thank you very much, when I get off this godforsaken island, out of your life, and back where I belong."

His words hurt. She knew they were designed to. She knew something else. She wasn't the only one running away from problems. He was running scared. Scared of her. Scared of his feelings.

"And where, exactly, do you belong?"

He was silent for a very long time. "Anywhere but here."

Swallowing back the pain, she asked softly, "Then why *are* you here? Why did you bother to come after me?"

His eyes were hard and cold when he faced her. "Dammit, Joanna. Hasn't it gotten through that stubborn red head of yours that you could have died out there?"

The anguish in his voice told her what he refused to put into words. "And you would have cared," she said, bravely holding his gaze. She stepped toward him. "You don't like it, but you would have cared."

Hands bracing the air between them as if to stave her off, he backed away, away from her, away from the truth of her words, and away, she knew, from his feelings.

"Yes," he said finally, sounding as if he'd run to hell and back trying to avoid the admission. "I would have cared."

Then he turned his back on her once more, closing the subject with as much finality as if he'd closed and locked a door.

Five

Adam concentrated on building the fire. He added tinder slowly and methodically until he was convinced he was in control again. And then he heard the rasp of her zipper going down. He laid the next log with a shaking hand. The sound of her wet clothes hitting the floor behind him brought his head up and sent his pulse racing.

For a vivid, heart-lurching second he recalled the way her slim frame had felt wedged between him and the wall. Cold and wet as she'd been, her small body had warmed his blood. And she was right, damn her. It had been a woman's body that had made his hard with wanting. A woman's breast he'd caressed.

That woman was just a foot away, his for the taking. He forced himself to picture her elfin face. A woman who looked that young and innocent had surely never been with a man. Especially not a man like him. Knowing it was futile, he struggled to place her in that niche in his mind reserved for puppies and children. She was neither, though, and with each passing moment, he became far too aware of that.

What she was, he acknowledged with an acceptance knotted with longing, what he'd known from the moment he'd laid eyes on her, was everything missing in his life. And he would be everything wrong in hers.

She'd despise him for it, but the only good thing he could do for her was push her away. If he didn't, she'd end up hating him more.

He turned abruptly to face her, relieved beyond measure to find her draped from neck to bare feet in his gray sweatshirt and sweatpants. Avoiding her huge, hurting eyes, he found a pair of his socks among the heap of clothes on the floor. He tossed them to her, then stoically set out the thermos of coffee and the food he'd snagged from her kitchen.

"Eat," he ordered.

Turning up the wick in the lantern, he took stock of the cabin. Though fairly clean, it had seen better days and years of wear. Tattered curtains that may have once been blue stirred slightly as the wind continued to rattle the multipaned windows. Rough cut knotty pine paneled the interior walls and peaked ceiling of the single room that served as kitchen, bedroom, and living area. A braided rag rug covered the bulk of the worn pine floor. The stone fireplace, thank God, was proving to be functional. Already it was stealing the chill from the room.

He walked to one corner and dragged a protective covering from a stack of bedding. Grimly determined, he tugged the two single mattresses in front of the fire, laid them side by side, and covered them with blankets and the sleeping bag.

Only then did he turn to her and deal with the most immediate problem. She was in shock, shaking so hard, the coffee was about to slosh over the side of the thermos mug.

He pried the mug from her hand, led her to the bed on the floor, and eased her down. He fed the fire, then in silence stripped off his own wet clothes. Knowing she needed his body heat to warm her, he crawled into the bed behind her. He pulled her against him, closing his mind to the feel of her.

"Adam . . . I'm s-sorry I g-got you into this m-mess."

"Shhh. Just . . . shhh," he whispered, hearing the tears in her voice and the gruffness in his. "Go to sleep, little girl. We'll deal with it in the morning."

Trusting and trembling, she snuggled against him. In a few minutes, she fell into an exhausted sleep.

Hours passed before Adam even dared to close his eyes. Hours in which he felt her thaw, and stir and shiver against his warm body. Hours of sweet agony as he lay behind her hard as stone, trying not to think of the mat velvet feel of the skin beneath his sweatshirt, the small perfect shape of her breasts, the dusky brown tightness of her nipples.

The wind rattled the windows. The woman sighed in her sleep. And Adam Dursky weathered his own private storm.

Morning dawned gray and dismal. The rain had stopped but the wind, if anything, had worsened. It beat like an angry fist against the little cabin. When Adam parted a curtain to look outside, he could see it had whipped the lake into an even more aggressive frenzy than the night before.

The rustle of the bed covers told him Jo was awake. Sensing her gaze was focused on him, he turned to face her. How many days, he wondered, could he make it without touching her?

She sat up, tousled and mussed, her hair a wild curling mane about her face. She looked a little battered, a little bruised, and entirely too vulnerable. Entirely too sexy.

His stomach muscles clenched. Her stomach growled. Embarrassed, she covered it with her hand, then flinched in pain.

"Sounds like you could do with some breakfast," he said.

"I'm fine."

He snorted. "And I'm the tooth fairy."

She looked away, plucking nervously at the downy sleeping bag.

"When were you planning on telling me about your hand?"

Her gaze, full of denial, snapped to his. The warning in his eyes must have made her think better of it. In the end, she shrugged. "I wasn't."

Watching her, he made a decision.

"About last night . . ." He paused as he sensed her preparing for another lecture. "I didn't know if I was going to live to see today. And until I found you here, I wasn't sure you were either. I'm sorry for the rough handling. I was way out of line. Like I said . . . chalk it up to a renegade surge of adrenaline. You scared the hell out of me, Red."

She blinked hard and looked away.

"But I didn't have to be such a bastard about it."

Hunkering down before her, he tentatively brushed her cheek with his knuckles. Heat shimmered along his fingers as he connected with her petal-soft skin. He dropped his hand quickly. "We're not out of this yet. There's no sign of a let-up in the wind, so we may be stuck here for a while." More gently, he added, "If we're going to make it through this without doing each other in, we'll have to call a truce of sorts."

She drew the sleeping bag closer to her breast. "I didn't know we were at war."

A muscle in his jaw flexed. He stood and looked

down at her. "No war. Just a major skirmish or two."

That finally earned him a smile. A small one. That a tomboy floundering inside his sweats could trigger such protective instincts in him no longer surprised him. That that same tomboy could have him itching to crawl back under the covers and teach her the fine points of seduction almost cost him his voice.

"Now, will you give me your hand?"

Without hesitation, she extended it. A peace offering.

With much hesitation, he took it. War fleetingly seemed the better option. Concern overshadowed hesitancy, however, when he realized the extent of the damage.

He swore softly. "Dammit, Jo, it's broken."

"I've suspected as much," she said through clenched teeth.

Gentle as he tried to be, he sensed it took all of her will not to flinch as he prodded her palm. She'd broken the bone just below her thumb. He gave her a sharp look. "Why didn't you say something about the pain?"

"What's to say? It hurt. Wailing about it wasn't going to make it better."

She was as stubborn as the aspen that bent but refused to break to the force of the wind. She dug in her heels the same way they put down roots and somehow gained a finger hole in the rock. He'd always thought of himself as rock hard, at least where giving in to emotion was concerned. Leave it to her to teach him different. "See if you can move your thumb."

She sucked in a harsh breath. It was the only sign that she'd tried.

"That's good. Easy. Don't push it." He sat back on his heels, ran his hand across his mouth, and broke into a cold sweat considering what he was about to do to her. There was no point in waiting. "Okay, Red. Now would be a great time to lay some of your colorful vocabulary on me. I've got to set this and it's going to hurt like hell." He jerked her thumb hard, setting the break before either of them had any more time to think about it.

She made a surprised and anguished sound, then turned deathly pale. Tucking her head tight to her chest, she let out her breath on a slow, tortured moan.

"It's okay. It's okay now," he crooned, agonizing over her pain. "It's over. Hold on while I splint it. It'll give you a little protection and ease some of the ache. You still with me, Red?"

She nodded jerkily.

"That's my girl." He squeezed her shoulder, then quickly made a splint by wrapping a wood chip in gauze from the first-aid kit. Carefully, skillfully, he bound her hand.

"You're very good at that."

So glad to hear her voice close to normal, he commented without thinking. "A lot of my buddies got hit in 'Nam. Medics were in short supply. You learned fast under fire how to treat any number of—" He stopped midsentence, catching himself. His gaze met hers over their joined hands. "Let's just say I got good at a lot of things."

Her eyes were full of questions. To her credit, she didn't ask one.

He tied off the gauze and inspected his work. "How does that feel?"

"Good. It feels good."

"It feels like hell, but give it a little time and the pain will ease." He checked the wrap. "Not too tight?"

She shook her head.

"I saw some aspirin in here somewhere," he said, rummaging around in the first-aid kit until he found them. "Why don't you take a couple to help knock the edge off?"

"No thanks. I'm fine."

"You're so fine, you're shaking like a small leaf in a big wind. Come on, tough guy. Doc Dursky says take 'em anyway. They'll reduce the swelling. Might even help the bruises you're bound to have from the beating you took on the water."

She reluctantly held out her left hand. "Thank you. I'm not used to having someone fuss over me."

And he wasn't used to fussing over anyone. He didn't want to get used to it either. It felt too good. Rising, he poured a cup of cold coffee for her, then watched as she tossed down the aspirin.

"How old are you anyway?" he asked out of the blue. Immediately, he regretted it. He could see in her eyes that she was remembering another time when he'd asked her that same question. He hadn't expected an answer then, and she hadn't expected his kiss.

"I'm old enough," she answered with a tight smile, "that it'll be a cold day in hell before I'll ever forgive you for calling me 'little girl' or 'kid.' I was twenty-six in August."

She looked pleased that she'd shocked him. And he was pleased that her spirit was returning.

"Your twenty-six years stacked up against my forty-one still makes you a kid in my book. And that stunt you pulled yesterday reeked of a spoiled adolescent trick."

Blinking hard, she stared at her coffee. "It's the only home I've ever known, Adam. It hurts knowing that I'm going to lose it again."

He tried to ignore the devastation in her voice and the tightness in his chest. "Maybe it just wasn't in the cards."

Drawing a deep breath, she gathered herself. "Yeah. Maybe."

Knowing he had to get away from her before he did something stupid, like drag her into his arms and love away her hurt, he shrugged into his rain gear and jerked open the door. "I'm going to check on your kayak and the boat, see if there are enough pieces left to put together something that will float."

"Adam?"

Her soft voice stopped him. He didn't turn around until she repeated his name, and when he did, a knot the size of Alaska seemed to have lodged in his throat.

"Thank you."

He grunted something that he hoped passed for, "Forget it," and headed out the door.

It was like a disease, Jo thought as he slammed the door behind him, this feeling that crept over her. It consumed her heart, her soul, and in the midst of a very real threat to her life, it consumed her thoughts. Its name was Adam. And it appeared to be incurable.

She rose slowly from her bed on the floor, more aware than ever of the beating she'd taken in the storm. Walking stiffly to the window, she watched Adam hunch his shoulders against the wind and make his way slowly through the woods to the shore.

He was a solid, unbendable object as he faced the wind alone. He'd made it clear last night with hard words and this morning with soft ones that there was no future for them together. Alone and hurting, she saw that now, and she saw the wisdom of his decision. He was there on borrowed time. She'd always known that, but had lost sight of the truth somewhere along the way.

Still a little shaky, she pressed her forehead against the cool windowpane. Steve's news had been a grim reminder of the fickleness of fate. Fate had brought Adam to her. It would also take him away . . . just as it had taken away everything that had ever been important to her. Her mother, her father, Shady Point.

Well, her problems weren't his and she wasn't going to solve them by moping. She turned away from the window, determined to make it easier on both of them. Adam was right. As long as the wind held, they were stuck here. Even if his boat was repairable or her kayak was seaworthy, it would be foolish to venture out on the lake when it was this rough. And it was a sure bet no one else would be out on it either. Besides, it might be days before anyone would miss them. When they did, and *if* they put it together that they were stranded somewhere on the lake, there were miles of shoreline and dozens of islands to search. That Adam had found her was a remarkable twist of fate.

There was that word again, she thought, and thanked God he'd given her one more measure.

Feeling exhausted, she rummaged around the small cache of food he'd brought and nibbled on a cookie. Then she lay back down and fell into a fitful sleep.

Jo awoke to the scent of fresh-brewed coffee and another trial. A fluttering excitement careened through her breast as she opened her eyes and became totally engrossed in the sight of Adam Dursky at his bath. A sense of decency should have kept her from staring. Decency, however, had to take a backseat to fascination. She lay perfectly still, knowing he was unaware that she watched him.

Stripped to the waist, his jeans low and snug around his hips, he stood before a small mirror hung on a nail above a tin washpan, his weight, as she was now so used to seeing it, slung on one long powerful leg. His blond head was wet and recklessly tousled from a recent washing. A single glistening water droplet trickled from under the towel looped around his neck and tracked slowly downward between his shoulder blades.

Watching with acute awareness, Jo held her breath as the pearly moisture drizzled down the long smooth length of his spine and slipped beneath the waistband of his jeans.

What the pale lantern light hadn't revealed last night, the daylight streaming through the windows did. He was every inch a male. Every smooth muscled movement, every tightly sculpted angle, spoke of strength and assurance.

Swallowing thickly, she wondered at his strength beneath the satin sheen of his skin . . . and at the thin scar that hugged his ribs just above his waist and disappeared around the front of his torso.

She felt a rush of pure arousal, but nipping at its heels was a niggling guilt. She snapped her gaze to the mirror and his reflection. He still didn't realize she was watching as he picked up a razor—Lord only knew where he'd found it—and started shaving.

The cords of his neck stretched taut as he scraped the blade from the hollow of his throat to the tip of his chin. After performing the same ritual on his cheeks and upper lip, he rinsed the razor and set it aside. Gripping both ends of the towel, he scrubbed away the leftover lather before tending to the telltale nicks on his face and neck.

Watching him, she thought of the hard-edged perfection of male models who decorated the pages of magazines, advertising everything from musky after-shave to golden whiskey to brokerage firms. There was something more substantial, though, more honest about Adam's bearing than glossy good looks.

He possessed the rough, brawny look of a construction worker, slim hips, long legs, and straining muscle. And there was a mind behind those piercing eyes. That aspect of Adam Dursky was as compelling as his beauty.

She shifted restlessly under the blankets, and her rustling movements drew his attention. He spared her a glance over his shoulder.

"Well, hello," he said, then buried his face in the towel for one last swipe. With his back to her, he shrugged into a soft flannel shirt.

"Hi," she managed as an interesting aroma of soap and cedar smoke from the fire wafted across the cabin.

She sat up slowly and watched as in a uniquely male gesture, he unzipped his fly and tucked the long shirttails into his jeans. She shivered and wondered how she would get through the next few days.

"Whoever stayed here last was kind enough to leave a few essentials," he said. "Soap, the razor. And there's enough cut wood to last the winter. Oh, and I found some food, besides the coffee." He stopped what he was doing to pour her a cup from the old metal pot on the wood cookstove. "There's a fruit cellar out back. Not a lot of variety, but it should get us by for a while. How do you feel about peaches?"

"Peachy."

He chuckled. "I was hoping you'd say that."

His gruff laugh made her remember the way he'd been the night before. Rough as coarse sandpaper, then gentle as spring rain when he'd held her.

Shaking the memories off, she threw back the covers. He was right there with a steadying hand to help her to her feet.

"Easy, now. You're bound to be a little lightheaded."

He didn't know the half of it. "Adam, I'm fine,"

she insisted. "You can quit fussing over me like I'm an invalid. Last I knew, stupidity wasn't a crippling condition."

He smiled again. "You weren't stupid. You were just scared."

"Yeah, well. The end results were the same." She moved to the fire. "You might want to check those tins on the shelf over there. My guess is they're full of crackers and some soup stock. Although the Larsons don't make it to the lake like they did when I was little, their son does. He keeps the cabin well stocked and usually tries to get up here before the end of October each year for one last long weekend."

"Jackpot," Adam said after hauling down the tins. He found everything from the crackers and soup stock, to powdered milk and powdered eggs. There was even some biscuit mix. "I'll have to find some way to thank the Larsons' son. It may not be McDonald's, but we won't starve. And these old moccasins I found in that chest of drawers are a damn sight more comfortable than my soggy boots."

It was her turn to smile. It came more easily than she'd expected.

"What's the news on the boat and my kayak?" she asked in an attempt to take her mind off the way he looked, all fresh scrubbed and solicitously concerned.

"It's not good. The boat's a total loss. The kayak is in better shape, but the hull is cracked. I'm afraid it's going to take someone more skilled than me to repair it."

Silence hung like a heavy cloud as they both digested the impact of that information. It meant they were stuck there until someone realized they were missing.

"Joanna."

She raised her head.

"Don't beat yourself over the head about this. We'll be fine. We'll get by."

"Yeah," she said, turning back to the fire. "We'll get by." But would they survive the days and nights alone with only the fire and the wind to distract them?

"You've been holding out on me, Dursky," she said an hour or so later as she sniffed appreciatively at the vegetable soup simmering on the stove. "It appears that you can cook."

"Throwing dried . . . what'd you call them?"

"Legumes."

"Yeah, legumes and dehydrated potatoes and carrots in a pot of boiling water hardly constitutes cooking."

"It's close enough for me. It smells wonderful."

"The proof will be in the tasting, and it's still a couple of hours away from being soup."

So far so good, Jo thought. They were both becoming excellent players in their little game of "let's pretend there's nothing between us but friendship." The rules were becoming more difficult to follow, though. Adam had managed to slip outside several times on the pretense of chopping wood or whatever other excuse he could dream up to get away from her.

But the heated looks, the telling glances, the quick flinches at each accidental touch were becoming harder to ignore.

And for Jo, the worst was yet to come. Just before he'd come in to make the soup, she'd slipped into her dry jeans, shirt, and sneakers and taken a much-needed trip to the outhouse. Unfortunately, she couldn't walk around in unzipped jeans and untied sneakers all day.

"I—I hate to ask this." She swallowed, then looked toward the ceiling and closed her eyes. "Oh, hell." She groaned and gestured toward the zipper of her jeans with her splinted hand. "Could you?"

Her exasperated plea cracked the frown of indifference he'd so carefully arranged on his face. He shook his head, scratched his jaw, and let a smile take over.

"Come here, little girl who can take care of herself. Let the big bad man zip up your pants."

"In your ear," she groused with a theatrical roll of her eyes.

She raised her shirt to give him access. He was laughing, but his hands, she noticed, were shaking as he zipped her up snugly.

He glanced down. "Your shoes too?" he asked. "Although judging by the look on your face, I'm not sure your pride can take it."

She returned his grin with a long-suffering look, muttered an oath under her breath, and held out her foot.

That taken care of, Jo decided to make herself scarce. Adam was making the effort to be friendly, and the very least she could do was see to it that he didn't have to stumble over her every time he turned around.

A walk would do her good, she thought, and set out toward one of her favorite spots on Jug. In the aftermath of the storm, the island was redolent with the damp musty scent of decaying leaves, forest loam, and crisp autumn air.

As she hiked through the forest, she thought of the resort. The threat of losing it still haunted her. And she thought of Adam. Of what haunted him and kept him so guarded against his feelings for her. He'd made reference to Vietnam, and his memories had obviously touched a deep pain within him. She'd seen it in his eyes. Without words, he'd told her more about himself than he realized.

He was a private man, a loner who asked for

neither help nor sympathy. The one thing she could do for him was respect his privacy. Yet the more she knew of him, the harder it was to keep her distance.

In the nippy wind, she made the short hike through the woods in record time. A jutting peninsula of solid white rock rose to the highest point on the island, affording her a view of the bay and the eagle's nest high in the pine across the inlet. By the time she reached it, gray sky had given way to blue. The rock was already sun warmed beneath her bottom as she settled down. She drew her knees to her chest and linked her arms around them.

The eagles didn't appear to be in residence. She knew they'd be close by, though, cruising the heavens like graceful gliders in search of food for their brood. The proud birds would hunt the lake land until mid-November, then migrate to a fairer climate. Their return in April always marked the end of a long winter, promising that a spring thaw would soon follow.

Wondering what spring had in store for her, she didn't hear Adam approach.

"It's very pretty here."

His voice behind her was a welcome surprise. Too welcome.

She shielded her eyes against the sun and smiled up at him. "For a man with a bad leg, you sure can sleuth your way around a forest."

He hunkered down beside her and stared out over the blue waters of the bay. "Must be the moccasins."

She glanced down at the soft leather covering his feet, then up at his golden head. She smiled. "If you're trying to tell me you're part Indian, forget it. No self-respecting Chippewa brave would be caught dead with all that blond hair."

"Heap big no-no, huh?"

His sullen delivery of the ridiculous question forced a chuckle. "The biggest."

They shared an unexpected and comfortable quiet while the sun warmed their backs and the top of their heads.

"How're you doing?" he asked, nodding toward her hand.

She held it out for his inspection. "Fine. It really feels a lot better. Thanks."

She itched to ask the same about his leg, but she didn't. And she wouldn't, no matter how badly she wanted to know.

She couldn't erase from her mind the picture of him kneeling before her to tie her shoes. His big hands had been so gentle. Nor could she shake the flood of tenderness she felt for this strong proud man who wasn't about to let her face her problems alone.

Adam watched the questions play across her delicate features. He sensed her desire to ask them, and he admired the fact that she didn't.

She was totally unassuming. She didn't inundate him with questions. She kept to herself, spoke when she was spoken to, and generally made every effort to stay out of his way. He liked that about her. He respected, too, her ability to adapt to their enforced exile. Like him, she was a loner. She knew how to be on her own.

He realized, as well, the extent of the fear that had pushed her out on the lake yesterday.

He watched her now, all glowing tresses and creamy skin as she closed her eyes and let the sun have its way with her. He hated to disturb her, but he'd come for a reason.

"I could use your help with something. Are you up for it?"

Her eyes opened. "Sure."

Something warm and wonderful filled his chest. Her immediate affirmation of trust stirred feelings he hadn't allowed for a very long time. Not for years. Not since Annie.

He rose slowly, then extended his hand and helped her to her feet. Was she for real, this woman with the face of an innocent and the unqualified trust of a lifelong friend?

Too long he stared into those spring-green eyes, marveling at the way the sunlight played across the amber gold of her thick lashes. Too long he held her small fragile hand in his callused palm and wondered at the feel of her fingers trailing across his bare skin.

In the space of a heartbeat something had been set into motion, something inevitable, unstoppable, and totally wrong. He wanted her with an urgency he hadn't felt in years. Standing there, with limited knowledge of the pale supple body wrapped in a baggy shirt and tight jeans, he wondered if he'd ever felt a rush of desire this strong.

He didn't understand what had triggered it. He only knew that he had to fight it.

It was Jo who finally had the presence of mind to break whatever it was that had gripped them and held them suspended.

"Is there a chance you'd feed me first?" she asked, breaking a silence that had become too expectant. "This business of staying out of your way has worked up my appetite."

He let his gaze drift over her face, then replied in a husky rasp, "Some appetites do need to be fed, don't they?"

She stared at him boldly. "And others?"

Sanity returned on the wings of her breathy question. He released her hand as if he'd just realized he still held it. "And others, being what they are, shouldn't be fed at all. Come on," he said gruffly. "Let's go do something about yours."

Six

The cabin steps needed repair and he'd found some rough tools in a shed out back. Adam had reasoned that the physical labor would provide him with a release, give him something to do with his hands. And it seemed like a small payback to the people whose cabin was providing his shelter.

He fed Jo, then put her to work with him. At the time, it had seemed like the safest course of action. As time passed, however, he questioned the wisdom of his decision.

He turned to grab another peg and became fascinated by the color of her hair. That was when he'd known he was in trouble.

Deep russet by the fire glow, and amber-gold in the sunlight, the heavy mass fell in feather-soft waves to well below her waist. He stared, spellbound as the sun played with the highlights, having a field day with the color.

He knew what it felt like wet. It had substance and texture and the delicate strength of fine silk thread. He was speculating about the feel of it dry and shining and slipping through his fingers, when with a quick toss of her head, she flipped the entire length over her shoulder and out of her way. Strand by strand, like sand sifting through an hour glass, it slipped free again until the whole glorious mass was back in her eyes.

The expectant look on her face made him realize he was staring . . . and that he'd been mesmerized by what he'd seen.

This had to stop, he told himself. This preoccupation, this adolescent fascination that was fast becoming an obsession. She may not be a kid, but he was damned near old enough to be her father. And he sure as hell didn't need the kind of headache involvement with her was certain to bring.

"Got it?" he asked as he lifted a porch step into place.

"Got it."

Jo managed to hold the wood steady by pressing her hip against the frame and her good hand under the board.

"My father used to make dock chairs out of rough cedar," she said, then caught herself when she realized she'd been enjoying the memory. "How did you learn to work with wood?"

"Trial and error mostly. And John and I used to spend a lot of time together in his little shop."

She said nothing. Her hair fell across her face again, hiding her reaction. He experienced an immediate sense of loss and covered it with irritation.

"Isn't that annoying?" he asked, nodding toward her hair. "How do you ever get anything done with it hanging in your face all the time?"

She gave him a little one-shoulder shrug. "Takes two hands to braid it."

Disgusted with his outburst, he forced himself to take a calm breath. "Hold on a second."

He tossed the hammer to the ground and rose stiffly. He'd spent more time than his leg was accustomed to crouched close to the ground. He limped over to the tree where he'd hung his jacket and with one tug slipped free the string that ran through the casement of the hood.

"This ought to do the trick."

She straightened and presented her back to him. Slowly he reached out and gathered the heavy mane in his hands . . . and the fascination began again.

Her hair was like nothing he'd ever touched before. Soft as down, fragrant as an autumn morning, it seemed alive with an energy of its own. He couldn't help it. He sifted it through his fingers, combed it away from her neck, held the weight of it in his big hands. The experience was an artful seduction of his senses, sensual and slow and impossible to fight.

"It's beautiful," he murmured raggedly, tempted to bury his face in the spun gold.

She stood very still, her slim shoulders tense. "You were right the first time. It's a nuisance."

"Well," he said hoarsely, so close that his breath stirred the fine strands clinging to her neck. "This ought to help."

With more determination than skill, he gathered the heavy mass and tied it together at the nape of her neck. His hands dropped lightly to her shoulders as he studied the clumsy job he'd done. "How's that?"

"Much better. Thanks." She faced him. "It was getting hot."

He felt her shiver despite her comment. His body responded with a burning warmth of its own. Too aware of that heat, he dragged his gaze away from hers, only to have it snag on the slender column of her throat where a light sheen of perspiration clung like dew.

Her skin was delicate. His hands were not. Yet he ached to touch her there. Gently, he framed the fragile tendons of her neck with long, work-roughened fingers. Skimming his thumbs across her skin, he drew away the glistening moisture, then studied the spot he'd just caressed. He swallowed, enthralled by the faint rhythm of her pulse beat. He wanted to press his lips there, to taste the salt and the sweat and the sweetness of her.

The voice of reason growled at him, warning him he was acting like a fool. He let his hands fall away. "Let's get back to work."

Though her eyes were soft and questioning, she bent back to her task.

They worked quietly the rest of the afternoon, keeping words and looks to a minimum. Accidental contact was pointedly ignored. Adam sensed she was struggling with the same tenuous control that he was. The guarded way she looked at him, the silence that spoke of her uncertainty, all indicated the extent of her tension.

By the time he'd finally hammered the last peg into place, he was in a rare mood, fueled by his frustration. He needed to put some distance between them before he did something they'd both have cause to regret.

Gathering the hand tools, he mumbled his thanks, then handled this problem much as he had handled other problems in his life of late. He walked away from it. Without a word or a backward glance, he strode off into the woods.

Jo stood, watching him go. A lump lodged in her throat. The heaviness in her chest pressed hard as she remembered the feel of his long, strong fingers tying her hair with such gentleness, of how those hands had caressed her.

From the beginning, she'd been too aware of his physical presence. His brusquely executed escape told her he was wanting too. The dawning realization stunned her. The wonder of it astounded her. Yet as she stood there, bathed in the autumn sunlight and the knowledge that a man like that could want her, the why of it ceased to matter.

She knew that when she left this island, she would leave a different person than when she came.

Walking slowly into the cabin, she looked at his bed where he'd moved it into the corner. She looked at her own in front of the fire. And she wondered if another night would pass before he came to her . . . or before she went to him.

New resolve and old regrets marked each footstep as Adam approached the cabin a couple of hours later. Control was critical. It was the only thing that would keep him from embarking on a journey that could only end in pain. She was innocent and clean. He was jaded by experience and soiled with the sins of his profession. He was going to stay the hell away from her.

Then he saw her and resolve snapped like the twigs beneath his feet.

She looked every bit of sixteen years old as she sat at the top of the cabin steps, bathed in the vibrant rays of the setting sun. Her feet were perched on the rung below her, her forearms crossed over her knees. Despite his determination to remain distant, he wondered what it would have felt like to steal her first kiss.

There was nothing good he could give her, and there was so damn much he could take away. He vowed again that he wouldn't touch her. But the hesitant smile that broke across her face when she saw him shook both his purpose and conviction.

"Hi," she said softly, her eyes shining with a guilelessness he doubted he'd ever known.

"Hi," he grunted, and forced himself up the steps and past her into the cabin.

"I heated up the soup if you're hungry."

"Fine." He closed the door and leaned back

against it, trying to forget the look of bewilderment that had clouded her eyes. He hissed a vivid expletive under his breath. Wasn't it better to leave her wondering than wounded? And that was exactly how he'd leave her if he got close enough to touch her again.

"This from a man who once prided himself on control," he muttered in disgust as he slammed around in the cupboard looking for a bowl. He found one and filled it. Propping his elbows on the table, he hunched over his supper like an angry bear guarding his last pot of honey. He'd shoveled down two mouthfuls when he stopped, drew a deep breath, and dropped his spoon into the bowl.

He flattened his forearms on the table and looked toward the door. Who the hell was he mad at? Her? Not fair, Dursky.

He strode across the room and opened the door.

"Have you eaten?" he asked, bracing his hand above him on the doorframe.

She didn't turn around. She just wrapped her arms around her legs and dropped her chin on her knees. "A little while ago."

He stared at the top of her head, working the muscle in his jaw. Sighing with resignation, he walked out onto the porch.

"Mind if I join you?"

She looked at him over her shoulder, clearly trying to read his mood. "I can go in, if you want the porch to yourself."

She started to rise. He stopped her with a hand on her shoulder. "No. Stay. I'd like the company." Before it was too late and before it started to feel too comfortable there, he pulled his hand away.

He eased to the bottom step and crossed his outstretched legs at the ankles. Propping his elbows on the step by her feet, he stared in the direction of the bay. The first evening star was a winking pinhole in the rosy blush of twilight. They watched in silence as dusk slowly relinquished its last bit of daylight to the gun-metal-blue of the darkening sky. Only the distant and profoundly constant wash of water infiltrated the quiet.

"How do you get used to it?" he asked, not looking at her. "The silence. The solitude."

He felt her shift on the step above him. "How do you get used to the sulfur and gas fumes of the city? I guess it's a question of what seems natural. If you grow up with solitude, you feel comfortable with it. I never got used to life in Minneapolis. I always felt misplaced there."

He twisted around to face her. "It must have been rough for you."

She looked off into the darkness, absorbed with something only she could see. When she met his eyes, her face was stripped of emotion. "I hated it. But I stayed because I had nowhere else to go. Aunt Grace and I were of the same mind about the decision. Neither of us wanted me there. It was the only thing we ever agreed on."

She stopped abruptly, clearly uncomfortable with his frowning attention.

"Doesn't exactly sound like you received an open-arms welcome."

"I'm sure it was a shock for her too," she said generously.

Too generously, he thought, unaccountably angry with some faceless old witch who could have provided a cushion instead of another blow.

"Anyway," Jo went on, "she put a roof over my head and clothes on my back, then pretended I didn't exist. I made it easy for her by staying out of her hair. The day after I graduated from high school I moved out. I worked my way through college, then got a job at an ad agency in St. Paul."

"And then?"

She shrugged. "And then I saved my money and this spring, I came home."

He was sure she wasn't aware of it, but when she said the word home, her eyes softened and all the tension eased out of her voice. At the same time, a corresponding warmth stole the last of his determination not to react to her. He didn't have to be her lover to be her friend.

"I guess you knew what you were talking about all along," he said thoughtfully.

"Excuse me?"

"You really do know how to take care of yourself."

She took his cue with a sparkle of mischief in her eyes. "By damn near getting myself drowned?"

He grinned, feeling too much pleasure in her smile. "So," he said speculatively, breaking the spell, "it was the solitude, or lack of it, that made you come back?"

"Yes, but more specifically, I came back because of Shady Point. I'd kept up-to-date with what was happening to the lodge through Steve and just bided my time until the right opportunity presented itself. This spring, I thought it had."

He stared into the night. "Life hasn't exactly been smooth sailing for you, has it?"

"It's definitely been a challenge."

"What now, Jo?"

She shrugged and lifted her chin. "Something will turn up. I'll get by."

"I'm sure you will," he said softly, then smiled to himself as he turned back to face the lake. "And may God have mercy on any mere male who might try to help you."

"I heard that," she said, joining the attempt to keep things light. "I may be stubborn, but I'm not stupid. If I truly need help, I accept it."

"But it hurts like hell, doesn't it?" He rose, brushed off the seat of his pants, and countered her silence with a gentle smile. "I bet I know something else that hurts."

She tilted her head warily.

"That skirmish you had with the lake last night was probably equivalent to hitting a truck broadside."

"I'm fine."

He laughed. "See? You'd chew nails before you'd admit that you're hurting. Your hand is broken, you took a beating in that storm, yet you'll sit there on your bruised pride and your black-and-blue butt and deny it."

"How do you know what color my . . . um, bottom is?"

He grinned, hearing the reluctant smile in her voice. "It was a lucky guess based on the way you moved all day."

He considered her with new appreciation. "You're too tough for your own good, Red. But there may be hope for you yet. That is, if you really can learn how to accept help when it's offered. Speaking of which, I've got a little surprise that just may make you feel better."

"Surprise?"

"Uh-huh. And while you're wondering what I'm up to, practice saying these three words: 'Thank you, Adam.'"

Leaving her with a puzzled frown, he slipped around to the back of the cabin.

That morning, when he'd rummaged around in the shed behind the cabin for tools, he'd found an old copper bathtub tucked in a corner. While she was napping, he'd washed it and left it to dry in the sun.

"What in the—Dursky!" she cried in delight as he hauled the tub up the steps.

"Patience, brat!" he ordered. When the tub was finally full of hot water and a warm fire was blazing in the hearth, he let her come inside.

She looked from the steaming tub to his face.

"For the little lady with the bruised pride and purple butt," he said gently.

Her eyes brightened with the threat of tears. "Thank you, Adam."

"You said that very well," he said in a gruff whisper. Ignoring that voice of reason, he lifted his hand to her hair. "Soak as long as you like. I'll just be outside. There's a T-shirt and a towel on the table."

The moon rose full and slow over the lake that night. Adam sat on the end of the point and watched it long after he was sure he wouldn't catch Joanna at her bath.

Then he watched it a little longer.

At last, he entered the cabin quietly. She was curled up in her bed sound asleep. His half-eaten bowl of soup had been cleared away, but the soup pot sat on the stove still simmering. A clean bowl and spoon were set on the table. Something foreign and warm tugged at his gut at her thoughtfulness.

He wasn't hungry. He sat at the table anyway and ate more soup while he watched her childlike body curl further into itself under her blankets. Then he stripped and slipped into the tepid water that smelled of soap and mineral and Joanna.

He washed slowly, envisioning her lithe body filling this space, imagining the water lapping at her breasts, seeing her soap-slicked hands skimming across her skin the way he ached to have his do.

He swore softly and shot out of the tub. *You're nothing but a horny old man,* he blasted himself silently. *And you're too damn old to be smitten! She's not for you, so for pity's sake, get a grip.*

He'd never wanted a woman so badly. And he'd *never* wanted a woman like her. He'd wanted women briefly and without feeling. He'd wanted them selfishly and without guilt.

But he wanted Joanna lingeringly and with as much feeling as he could wring from her languid limbs. He wanted her so he could bury his guilt deep inside her.

He toweled himself dry and whipped back the covers on his bed. Lacing his fingers behind his head, he stared at the ceiling, forcing himself to relax. The same disturbing thought presented itself over and over again, though. How many nights would pass before he went to her . . . or before she came to him? And where would he find the strength to tell her no?

Jo awoke with a start, her heart pounding frantically. She sat straight up, brushing the tumble of hair from her eyes as her sleep-drugged thoughts scrambled to connect with the sound that had roused her.

A tortured groan from the far side of the room brought her to her feet and to Adam's side.

"Adam," she whispered, dropping to her knees by his bed. She laid a hand on his forehead. It was beaded with perspiration.

"Adam, wake up," she said more forcefully. He moaned and threw his head from side to side. He was drenched in sweat, his blanket twisted in a knotted tangle around his hips where his clenched fists dug into the mattress.

She grabbed one shoulder with her good hand. "Adam." She shook him. "Adam, please, wake up!"

Stormy gray eyes snapped open. His glazed gaze darted wildly around the darkened cabin as he grabbed her wrist and jerked her hand away. He rolled out of bed and slammed her to the floor beneath him, pinning her arms above her head.

"A . . . dam . . ." she cried, struggling as he crushed her body with his weight. "Adam, you're hurting me. Adam . . . please. Wake up. It's Jo."

His breath beat hot against her face, stirring the hair at her temple. The fear and pain threaded through each shaky word must have brought him to his senses.

"Jo." He heaved a tortured sigh, his breathing rough. "Joanna. Oh, Lord. Did I hurt you?"

She shook her head, her heart beating erratically against his chest.

"God, Jo." Slowly, he released her wrists. Levering his weight onto his elbows, he cupped her face in his hands. A tear slid down her temple toward her ear. He groaned, caught the moisture on his thumb, then pressed his lips to the damp skin beneath the tear track. "Oh, Red, I'm sorry."

"You—you were having a nightmare."

He laid his forehead against hers and closed his eyes. "Yeah." He drew a ragged breath. Soothed by her nearness and the sweet fresh fragrance of her skin, he felt his breathing gradually slow, his pulse steadily lessen.

He'd frightened her, hurt her even, yet when he raised his head to look at her, her eyes were awash with concern. He hadn't felt that from a woman in years. In that moment, he knew he could trust her. With his deepest secrets. With the awful truths of his life.

Thanking fate or kismet or whatever powers that be for landing them together at this particular place and time, he smiled crookedly, apologetically, and brushed the hair back from her temples.

"You seem to have a penchant for getting manhandled by me."

Her eyes softened. He felt her body relax beneath him.

"You're the only man I'd let get by with this a second time." Her voice was deeper, huskier than he'd ever heard it.

Their gazes locked, and her soft smile faded. She stirred beneath him. Awareness was swift and explosive. The only thing between them was the sheen of perspiration coating his skin and the thin cotton T-shirt she'd worn to bed. He groaned, feeling an instant surge of arousal.

"Ah, Jo." He buried his face in the dewy skin at her throat, losing himself in her warmth. "You feel so damn good." He pressed a kiss against her skin knowing he should let her go. "So damn good . . ." He drew her closer. "And it's been so long since I've wrapped myself around anything but a bad dream."

Small, warm hands hesitated, then settled on his arms. Slowly, as if memorizing the texture, categorizing each muscle, she slid them up to rest on his shoulders. He shuddered and nipped the delicate hollow of her collarbone. "Send me back to my bed," he ordered raggedly, "while I still have the strength to leave you."

She arched her neck to give him better access. "Your bed is drenched in sweat," she whispered. "You can't go back there. Come to mine."

His heart stopped, then pounded in double time. Blood pulsed to his groin, rolling over sanity. He forced himself to look into her eyes. They were wide open, full of promise and passion and an innocence that demanded he stop."This is crazy, Jo."

"I know."

He kissed her cheekbone. Her lashes fluttered softly against his lips. "There's no future in this . . . for either of us." He scattered random kisses that begged her to go, yet enticed her to stay.

"I'm not asking for a future."

"Dammit, Joanna." He wrenched his mouth away from the drugging taste of her skin. "This isn't right. I'm old enough to be your father and you—"

She pressed two trembling fingers against his lips. "And I'm old enough to know it doesn't matter."

He held her gaze in the fire glow. "Are you sure?"

"I'm sure I want you. I'm sure I need you."

"You're sure now. Tonight. But what about tomorrow?"

She brushed back a damp lock of hair that tumbled over his forehead. "I'm not asking for tomorrow."

"Grabbing the wrist of her good hand, he pinned it to the floor above her head. "But you should be!" he bit out. "You should be. And I can't give it to you. You deserve more." He closed his eyes and clenched his jaw. "And I've got nothing more to give."

"You've given me your honesty. That's enough."

He shook his head, fighting to do what he felt was right, aching to do what he knew was wrong. "Joanna." He breathed her name on a sigh. "Are you . . . have you ever . . ."

"I'm not a virgin, if that's what you're afraid of. Look." She gave a small, defiant shrug of her shoulders, her passion suddenly reduced by doubt. "I didn't mean to pressure you."

He heard the hurt. Each word hit him like a gut punch.

"I—I thought we wanted the same thing," she went on. "If you're trying to find a graceful way to tell me you're not interested, don't worry about it."

She bucked under him, trying to roll him off and away.

He held her fast. She was incredible. Seductive in her innocence, bold in her declaration of need. Yet for all her self-assurance, she didn't realize the effect she had on him. He wanted her so badly, it hurt. He wanted to fill his hands with her round bottom, his mouth with her breasts. He wanted to gentle her, to fill her, to make her cry out in passion. He wanted her so bad, he feared he'd bruise her, physically and emotionally. "You don't know, do you? You don't know how desirable you are."

"I'm a realist. I've lived with this face for twenty-six years. It's the face the boys used to look past to get to the pretty ones. It's the face that prompted my friends to leave their dates with me for safe-keeping. It's not a face that elevates pulse rates and inspires heavy breathing."

He pressed her hand to the center of his chest where his heart pounded with his need for her.

"Feel this," he said gruffly. Framing her face in his hands, he forced her to look at him. "If my heart rate elevated any higher, we'd be talking cardiac arrest here. You do that to me."

Her lashes screened eyes grown cloudy with questions. "Then why are you turning me away?"

Her vulnerability was heartbreaking. Breath-taking. Angered that he didn't have the will to stop the madness, he levered himself above her and offered a reason to send him back to his bed. "Because you don't have any idea what you're getting into. Because if I don't stop now, I'll settle for nothing less than all of you."

He crushed his mouth to hers, intent on proving his point. Bracketing her head in his palms, he forced her lips apart with the not-so-gentle pressure of his thumbs. His tongue pillaged and plundered the warm recesses of her mouth with a violence intended to frighten her. But if anyone was frightened, it was he, by the urgency with which he wanted to take her and by the trusting pliancy with which she responded.

He jerked way and stared deep into her eyes. They were glistening with excitement and a fear she couldn't quite conceal. Her lips were parted and swollen from his kiss. Against his chest, he could feel her heart clamoring.

"Do you understand, now?" He ground his hips against hers, seducing her with his arousal even as he issued one final warning. "Do you understand what I want from you, Jo?"

She wet her lips with the tip of her tongue. "Yes."

"Oh, baby." He groaned."I don't think you do. You're so damn trusting, so naive about the appetites of a man like me. I've seen and experienced too much. I want it all, Jo. This is no sweet slap and tickle, no demure nocturnal interlude. I want you in ways you can't imagine."

"You'd never hurt me. Adam, listen to me. All my life I've had to think about tomorrow and the consequences of what I do today. Just once I want to take the moment and go with what feels right."

He lowered his mouth to her throat. "And all my life I've taken it as it comes, the consequences be damned."

She turned her face into his hair. "Then don't change on me now, Dursky. Please don't change on me now."

Just that fast, the battle was over.

If there was a surrender, it was his.

If there was defeat, it was sweet.

The trust in her eyes was devastating, and provocative, and so total, he promised himself she was right. He would never hurt her. If it took every shred of restraint, he'd make himself go slow with her.

He pressed a tender kiss on her brow, then eased away. Rising to his feet, he extended his hand and drew her up against him, wrapping her in his arms and holding her for a long, soul-searching moment.

Then he led her to her bed on the floor.

For all her earlier bravado, Adam sensed her

shyness and self-doubt returning. He stretched out full length beside her, propping his head on his palm and curling a finger under her chin.

"A boy might overlook this face," he said, "but a man never would."

Her lips parted, glistening. He touched them lightly with his own, finding them quivering and cool. "You taste wonderful."

Timidly, she lifted to him, extending the contact.

Smiling against her mouth, he deepened the kiss, rimming her lips with his tongue before delving inside, probing gently. "You must have had very stupid friends . . . or they had blind boyfriends."

This time it was she who smiled against his lips."You're very tactful, aren't you, Mr. Dursky?"

"You're very tasty, aren't you, Ms. Taylor?" He nibbled at the corner of her mouth before returning to its center and kissing her with an urgency that left him panting.

He trailed his hand unerringly down the length of her body, lingering over the cotton-covered tip of one breast. The sensitive nipple throbbed to hardness beneath his fingers. She moved restlessly against him when he lowered his hand to the tangle of silken curls between her thighs.

With trembling fingers he lifted the T-shirt over her hips and touched the velvet softness of her belly."Joanna." He groaned as his fingers slipped inside her waiting warmth and found her wet and wanting and ready for him.

She thrust upward against the pressure, moaning softly.

Swiftly moving over her, he parted her thighs with his knee and settled against her. "I wanted to take this slow," he said hoarsely.

But slow was beyond hope.

Need was beyond measure.

An appetite that for so long had been fed only by meager portions of nameless, meaningless encounters, gnawed with a hunger that demanded more than just his passion be sated. This was a woman whose name he would never forget, whom he feared would come to mean more to him than the next breath he drew, and whose face would haunt him the rest of his life.

"Joanna," he murmured as he probed, penetrated. He buried himself in her tight giving heat, and she arched to him. She moved with him. She wrapped her legs around him and rode with him in a rhythm as timeless as the lap of the water to the shore, to an end as fulfilling as the act of love was intended.

Seven

Carefully, so as not to wake him, Jo disengaged herself from the circle of Adam's arms. She sat up on the blankets beside him, tucked her knees to her chest and laid her cheek on her crossed arms. With rapt fascination, she watched him sleep.

Adam at bath had been captivating. Adam at rest was a miracle. His magnificent jaw was slack, his expression restful and thoroughly sated. She felt a swift and filling rush of elation. She was responsible for that look and for the wonderfully lethargic sprawl of his limbs.

Her gaze traveled the golden length of his body. How could all that power diffuse into such quiet slumber? How could all that strength give way to such careful loving? Even with her limited knowledge of the physical act of love, she sensed it had been a long time since he'd been with a woman. The urgency with which he'd taken her had been telling. He'd warned her that he could hurt her. It was then, as he'd issued his ardent warning, that she'd accepted the depth of her love for him. As she watched him now, with exquisite knowledge of his gentleness, she reaffirmed that fact. She did love him. Completely. Irrevocably. So much that she'd make sure he didn't feel obligated to stay.

She'd come to him with her eyes wide open. She'd offered herself out of need. But what she felt in the aftermath of their lovemaking was nothing so staple as need, nothing so fleeting as desire. It was a completion of sorts, a yielding of a spirit she'd held so rigid, she'd thought no man could bend it. Yet Adam, this private and sadly vulnerable man, had broken through a barrier she'd thought was impenetrable. Because of his own need, he'd reached deep inside her and uncovered feelings she'd intended to live a lifetime without.

He'd ask for her physical love with an unblinking honesty that included no offers of forever, just a need for the here and now. She'd accepted those terms willingly.

Tugging the T-shirt that smelled of Adam lower over her hips, she turned toward the fire. She added a piece of cedar to the embers, watching the flames catch hold. It was sad, she thought, that what had barely begun between them would end as abruptly as it had started. Only a precious few days separated reality from fantasy.

But it was life. It was *her* life, and she'd learned long ago not to expect any more from it. Anyone she'd ever loved had left her. Adam would be no exception. He wasn't hers to keep and treasure. He was fate's fleeting gift for what she'd gone through and gone without. She accepted it as her due and intended to savor each moment.

For however long they had, she would give and take with equal fervor. No questions asked. No promises extracted. She would be all to Adam he could want in a woman. She would take from him all she wanted from a man. In the process, they would both find their lives a little richer, the loneliness ahead a little easier to bear.

Brushing away a tear that tracked down her

cheek, she refused to give way to sentiment. She watched the fire, determined not to think about tomorrow, or next week, or next year. . . .

Adam awoke slowly from the druglike lethargy induced by making love to Jo.

Making love to Jo.

He sighed deeply and realized that was exactly what he wanted to do again. The warmth of her body against his own was painfully absent. Opening his eyes to a newly kindled fire, he found her silhouetted before it.

The fire glow framed her tiny body. The flames caressed her hair, haloing the long shining strands in hues of copper-and-autumn gold. He watched in fascination as a fire of his own reached a flash point.

She was so quiet. He wished he could see her face. Was she frightened? Was she sorry? Was she ashamed?

Or was she wanting him again, the way he had awakened wanting her?

Jo. What have I done to you?

Her shoulders were slightly bowed. Her slender hips, sheathed in the white cotton of his T-shirt, flared delightfully, evocatively. Toes as pink as a baby's cheek peeked out from under her gently rounded bottom. He wanted to take each one in his mouth, love each one with his tongue, and leisurely work his way up the length of her slender, giving body.

He wanted to pleasure her until she cried his name. And then he wanted to love her some more.

Jo. What have you done to me?

The first time he'd looked in her eyes, he'd known she possessed the ability to make him care again. It wasn't an emotion he could afford. He couldn't care, or feel, or ask more from a life that seemed determined always to leave him with less and wanting more.

When he looked at her, though, he wanted. And what he wanted was to lose himself again in the sweet wonder of her body. More than that, in the honesty of her responses, in the openness of her heart.

As he let his gaze travel the length of her back, he realized what an empty shell of a man he'd become. Time and circumstances had hollowed out his sense of purpose the way wind erodes fallow land. For years he'd been barren of emotions, empty of feeling.

She'd changed all that. She had filled him with her giving. Healed him with her trust. He felt like a long cold winter awakening to the warmth of a spring thaw. Like shadow solidifying into flesh. And he meant to give it all back to her.

He'd take her slowly this time, and in the taking he'd gift her with the sense of warmth she'd offered him.

Levering himself up on an elbow, he reached out to touch her hair. His newly enlightened flesh came alive as he held it in his hand. Amber silk floated through his fingers. "Are you all right?"

She nodded.

"Regrets?"

She looked back over her shoulder. Meeting his eyes briefly, she shook her head. "None."

If the relief had been sweeter, he would have died from it. Only days ago he'd seen her as a little girl, with a little girl's need for protection. But when she'd lain beneath him, she'd become all woman. It was a woman's eyes that had gone liquid with passion. A woman's body that had strained with need when he'd moved inside her. It was the woman he turned to now, jealous of the fire glow that caressed her body and tinged her skin with heat.

He rose to his knees behind her and touched his lips to her hair. Bracketing her shoulders with his hands, he pulled her against him.

She trembled.

"Do I frighten you?" Spreading his knees wide, he lowered himself behind her. The fine bones of her shoulder blades slid against his chest. Her hair flowed like cool silk against his skin as he couched her hips with his thighs and buried his face against her neck.

"No." She sighed as he draped her hair over her shoulder to make way for his mouth.

He fed on the slender column of her throat as he slid his hands down the length of her arms.

"You're shivering," he whispered as he captured her small-boned wrists. "Are you cold?"

"No," she murmured, sounding breathless. She pressed back against him, the fingers of her good hand digging into the muscle of his thigh.

He nipped the taut cords of her neck. "Hot, then?"

"Yes . . . Adam . . . What are you doing to me?"

He chuckled against the delicate skin beneath her jaw, and felt her shudder and yearn and stretch in one sensuous, sultry motion. "I'm seducing you, Red. And this time, I'm going to take it slow."

On their knees before the fire, her leaning back against him, he began loving her as slowly as he promised; as expertly as his experience had taught him; as purposefully as if he intended to make it his life's work. His hands, knowing and sure, stole downward to her waist, then dropped to cup and knead the curve of her hips.

"You're so soft here," he whispered. "And here. Raise your arms." He worked the T-shirt up over her head. "I want to feel you against me." Crossing his arms over her ribs, he filled his palms with the delicate weight of her breasts and pulled her snugly against him.

Her nipples pearled beneath his fingertips. "So sensitive. So responsive. Put your arms around my neck."

With complete trust, she obeyed, lifting her arms over her head and linking her wrists behind his neck. The movement thrust her breasts deeper into his palms. He felt as well as heard her breath catch as his fingers plucked and strummed and played against her skin.

"Ah, Jo," he growled, holding her against his heat with one hand and foraging lower with the other.

With a lambent touch, he feathered his fingers through her feminine curls, arousing her by degrees, teasing her body to a restless hunger. He nurtured a want that craved little persuasion, fostered a yearning that needed even less urging. She was a nucleus infused with passion, on fire with a desire to experience everything his touch implied, everything his husky whispers promised.

"Easy," he murmured, biting the curve of her shoulder. "Easy. Just go with it. Let it take you."

"Adam . . ." she cried as he parted and finessed and induced her feminine flesh to pulsing sensation. She strained against his hand, pressed her head to his shoulder, and unable to hold back, cried out as he stroked her. Her body was racked by tremors as with ultimate sensitivity to her needs, he lovingly, unerringly, brought her to a shattering climax.

"Sweet, so sweet . . ." he murmured against her skin, neither knowing nor caring if the moisture dewing her shoulder was left there by his kisses or by her own passion-borne perspiration.

He turned her in his arms and held her against his chest while she trembled.

"Adam . . . I've n-never . . ."

He smiled into her hair and held her tighter. "Never?"

She shook her head.

"Then we'll have to make up for some lost time, won't we?"

The gentle laughter in his voice brought her head up. He quelled her embarrassment with a kiss. "You were beautiful. Beautiful."

"I was loud." She groaned miserably and snuggled against him.

"Loud and lush and"—he brushed his thumb across her cheekbone and looking longingly into her eyes —"and I can't wait to hear your love sounds again. Lie down for me. Let me look at you."

The ardor in his eyes erased any remnant of embarrassment Jo might have felt. She lay back willingly, watching his eyes turn to a dark, smoky silver as he plumped both pillows beneath her shoulders and arranged her against them.

The light from the fire reflected the flame of his building desire. He knelt beside her and took her bandaged hand to his mouth. He kissed it tenderly, then laid it beside her head on the pillow. She watched in wonder as next he brought her unbandaged hand to his lips. He kissed her palm lingeringly, wetting it with his tongue.

Latent passion stirred back to life within her as he flicked his tongue between her fingers, then gently nipped the heel of her hand before laying it, too, on the pillow beside her head.

She was totally vulnerable, completely exposed to the building passion in his eyes, yet she'd never felt more secure. Secure in the knowledge he'd never hurt her. Secure in knowing that the wanting he felt for her was real.

His gaze burned across her body, singeing her flesh with its fire. She gathered herself as licking curls of sensation swirled from her breast to her belly and pulsed with heat between her thighs. Only moments ago she'd been sated, thoroughly, gloriously. Yet she wanted him again with a yearning that transcended reason, with a passion that defied comprehension.

"How did you get this way?" he asked, his tone thick with wonder. His dark hand covered her breast. Cupping her gently, he molded her breast with his palm, then circled the rosy aureole with his thumb.

She closed her eyes and shivered as her nipple crowned.

"You're so small and perfect. I love how you respond to me. Beautiful." Twisting at the hip, he lowered his mouth to hers for a lingering kiss.

"Beautiful . . ." he repeated on a groan. He wet the gentle ridge of her collarbone with his tongue, then dried her skin with his breath before moving on to trail moist kisses across her torso.

With his hands on either side of her, he braced his weight above her. "Open your eyes, Joanna. Open your eyes and see how pretty you are when I love you."

She met his gaze, stunned anew by what she saw there. Vivid with the heat of their shared passion, yet gentled by the way she had given herself to him so completely, his expression spoke of healing, and trust, and, though she didn't recognize it at first, of love.

Her heart rejoiced, then plummeted back to earth as her discovery was made bittersweet by the truth. Only in his eyes would she ever see the love that equaled what she felt for him. Only in his eyes would she know the depth of his feelings.

"I can't give you more than today," he'd said. She'd known he'd spoken the truth. Whatever ghosts haunted him, they had the power, not her. He wasn't free to love her. And he wasn't there to stay.

Through misty eyes she watched him lower his

head to her breast. Her heart aching, she witnessed the unqualified generosity of his loving until the passion he milked from her body transcended the pain.

She sighed his name as he pillowed his blond head between her breasts.

His tongue was bold and daring, his teeth shocking yet infinitely gentle. And his hunger was a fierce thing as he suckled, feeding from each pink-tipped bud, striving to sate an appetite that knew no limit.

His hunger fed her own. She pressed herself into his mouth, cupping his head in her hand and showing him with her caress how much she shared his need.

Sensual pleasure blended sweetly with an achingly tender emotion she'd never associated with lovemaking. Yet the nurturing yearnings she felt as he drew at her breast were intrinsically woven into the act of love. She felt protective and maternal as she cradled his head in her hands, and she held him until the ache to become one drove them both.

She guided his head to her mouth. When he moved over her, she welcomed him home. And when he finally filled her, she cried out with the joy of his possession.

He was virile strength and passion. She was melting warmth and yearning. Together, they were magic.

"Joanna," he whispered against her hair before he succumbed to the narcotic pull of sleep. "How am I ever going to leave you?"

She nestled deeper into his arms and went the same way he did. "How am I ever going to let you go?"

They slept the sleep of lovers until, stirred by the newness of each other and the undeniable awareness that they would soon part, they awakened to make love again.

The cover of darkness, diluted only by warming firelight, freed them to feel and experience without inhibitions. The night supplied what sleep provides for the subconscious mind. They hid in the darkness, playing by the fire glow. Cocooned by the intimacy of the isolation, they denied the existence of tomorrow.

There were no rules to restrain them. No rights to erect barriers, no wrongs to inflict guilt. There was only sensation and pleasure. Without words they acknowledged a void they both shared, then they filled it with each other.

The first faint traces of dawn mottled the morning sky with mauves and pinks and pearly gray when Jo awoke again. She looked lovingly down at the head pillowed on her stomach, the broad shoulders covering her hips.

Adam.

She sifted his golden hair through her fingers, smiling lazily when he reacted by cinching his arms tighter around her.

He was in the truest sense an intimate stranger, yet she'd never felt closer to another human soul. To have shared the physical act of love with him was a gift she couldn't yet comprehend. And one she wasn't ready to give up. Not yet.

"You're awake," he said sleepily. Turning his face into her stomach, he nuzzled her gently.

Submerged in his warmth and remembered passion, she managed to keep at bay the reticence she knew would eventually catch up with her.

"I'm awake," she murmured. "I'm not sure if I'm alive, though."

He chuckled, then snaked a hand across her ribs to coax a rosy nipple to an aroused peak.

"You're alive," he pronounced, sounding smug and sexy and arrogantly pleased.

She groaned, in awe of his ability to excite her with a touch. "I'm alive," she agreed breathlessly, trying to ignore the sensations he created as he dipped his tongue into her navel like a hungry bear delving for honey. "But am I well?"

Bracing his hands on either side of her hips, he levered himself up and smiled lazily into her eyes. "You are well. In fact . . ." He lowered his mouth to her breast and bestowed his first morning kiss there. "You are well . . . and good . . . Ummm . . ." His tongue circled, then swirled across her nipple. "Very, very good."

"And *you* are very, very strong."

He raised his head. Concern darkened his eyes. "Sore?"

This time her smile was smug. "Blissfully."

"I'm sorry."

She met his intense gaze, cupping his jaw with her palm. "I'm not. Last night . . ." She paused and had to look away so he wouldn't see the tears that came from nowhere and threatened to overflow. "Last night was wonderful. I've never felt such things. I didn't know there could be so much . . ." Again her voice trailed off, this time from sheer embarrassment.

"So much what, Jo? So much pleasure?"

Lowering her eyes, she nodded.

"Hey." He tipped her face to his with a knuckle under her chin. "The pleasure was mine."

What the night had hidden, the awakening dawn revealed. Despite her struggle to suppress it, uncertainty crept in with the light of day.

"I—I wish I could have been more . . ." She swallowed, unable to say the words.

"More what? More beautiful? Impossible. More responsive? No way."

"More experienced," she finally managed, hating the childlike defiance that edged into her voice.

He closed his eyes, drew a deep breath, then leveled her with a look so intense, her heart nearly stopped. "I didn't need your experience, Joanna. I needed you. And now that I've had you, I hate every scummy sonofabitch who touched you before I did and didn't know what they were giving up when they let you go."

The vehemence of his statement surprised them both.

Adam wrenched himself away from her. He grabbed a piece of wood and shoved it on the fire. It nettled him, this protectiveness he felt for her. He had no right. And he was no better than any other man she'd known. He wasn't absolved of his sins because he'd told her up front he wasn't going to stick around for the long haul.

The silence became a lurking presence in the room, overshadowing the uncut purity of the night they had shared. He didn't know how long he'd stared at the fire before she spoke.

"There was only one," she said softly.

He snapped his head around and threw her a puzzled look. "One what?"

He'd been a million miles away, Jo realized, thinking thoughts she'd never be privy to, reliving old angers that he might never forgive. It hurt that he'd so easily separated himself from her.

Suddenly angry at a life that gives so sparingly then takes away with such malicious pleasure, she answered him succinctly. "One scummy sonofabitch."

Whatever reaction she'd expected, it wasn't what she got. His slow, almost satisfied smile smoothed the briers from her battered ego and made her go all liquid inside. The warmth in his eyes took the hurt away.

"You really *do* have a nasty mouth for such a little girl, you know that?"

Prompted by the grin on his face and the teasing in his voice, she swung back to the lighthearted mood that had enfolded them when they'd awakened in each other's arms.

"You really think so?" she asked brightly, as if he'd just praised her with a lavish compliment.

"Yeah." He rounded on her menacingly. "And if you aren't going to do something about it, I am."

He lowered his body onto hers and framed her face with his hands.

"Is this the part where you wash my mouth out with soap?"

He grinned wickedly. "No, ma'am. I have other plans for your sweet little mouth. This is the part where I give up on reforming you and employ other methods of keeping you quiet."

"Adam—"

"Shut up," he ordered against her lips, then kissed her gently, tenderly. When the fun transcended quickly into passion, he tried to coax her mouth open with his tongue.

"Problem?" he asked when she didn't respond to his probing invitation.

"I believe you told me to keep my mouth shut."

"Ah . . . My mistake."

She looped her arms around his neck and shifted to accommodate his weight. "It takes a big man to admit his mistakes."

"And it takes a woman to point them out. Now open for me, Red . . . and the only thing I want to hear out of you for the next hour or so is a moan."

"Your bath is getting cold," Adam informed her much later that morning as she stretched and yawned and made a halfhearted effort to break loose of sleep. The lethargy that came from being thoroughly loved had settled in her limbs, coaxing her into a laziness foreign to her nature. The enticement of a hot bath, however, lured her further awake.

She sat up and smiled into the eyes of the only man who had ever kissed her good morning.

"You're dressed," she said with a glimmer of dismay that earned her a slow sexy grin.

Adam sat back on his heels, his gaze caressing her body. "And you're not," he replied in a gravelly rasp, wishing that the yearning he saw in her eyes would dull the lingering guilt he felt over stealing her innocence.

The sheet had slipped to her waist and lay hugging her hips. Her hair fell in a tangled skein down her back. One fiery lock ribboned across her chest, almost but not quite hiding one rosy nipple. Her breasts were swollen and taut, the pale ivory skin still rouged from the ardor of his loving.

He forced himself to stand up. "And if you *want* to get dressed sometime today, you'd best rouse yourself, or I'll be back between those sheets so fast, it'll make your head spin."

"Mine's already spinning."

She wasn't a flirt. That much had always been obvious. But this morning, feeling secure in the knowledge of his desire for her, she seemed born to the role. He'd awakened the woman in her last night and he loved watching her revel in the newness and excitement.

She met his eyes with a smoky invitation.

"Have mercy on me, woman." He laughed and tugged her to her feet. "I'm an old man."

"A regular old codger," she said, easing herself into the tub.

She made him feel like a randy young buck. God help him, he wanted her again. But when the hot water reached the delicate flesh of her femininity and she couldn't hide a wince of pain, he was immediately contrite.

He wouldn't embarrass her by commenting or apologizing. Instead he gathered her hair in his hands and draped it over the rim of the tub as she settled back with a blissful sigh. He knelt down and lathered his hands with the soap, then, indulging in a pleasure of his own, he began to bathe her.

"You have beautiful skin," he commented as she closed her eyes and relaxed under the smooth glide of his hands.

"I have freckles," she replied, sounding put out.

He smiled and soaped the length of each arm and back, enthralled by the delicacy of her fine-boned wrists. "Beautiful skin," he repeated, careful not to get her bandaged hand wet.

"Chalky white and subject to sunburn and rash."

He watched his soap-slicked hand caress the satin curve of her shoulder and thought again of the 'what ifs' that had started formulating sometime in the middle of the night. They'd multiplied rapidly while he'd prepared her bath and let himself watch her sleep. What if things were different? What if he were fifteen, even ten years younger? What if he didn't have to go back to Detroit to face his demons and settle some scores? What if they could just stay together forever on this island? What if he didn't have a problem that she had every right to abhor?

Regrets wouldn't change the facts. There was nothing to be done about what had already passed between them and before they'd met.

When he left her—and he *would* leave her, he forced himself to acknowledge that with a determination made weak by wanting—at least he would go with the knowledge that he'd convinced her she was a desirable woman.

He needed no such convincing. He became hard as stone when he lowered his hands beneath the surface of the water in search of the soap. She stirred slightly, causing the water to swell around her breasts, hovering near but not covering their rosebud tips.

He raised his hands slowly, sudsing those breasts. Her eyes opened at the same time his fingers seduced her nipples to erect peaks.

Unable to help himself, he leaned over her. With the tip of his tongue, he caught a runnel of water trickling down her breast, then lingered and licked and sipped.

Her sound of longing brought his head up.

"Well," he said, sitting back, "I guess that's enough of that."

She brushed her fingertips across his cheek. "I don't think I'll ever get enough of that." Embarrassment flooded her face. Averting her eyes, she sank deeper beneath the water.

She looked so small and vulnerable, he was again reminded of her childhood. "How did you lose your mother?"

She hesitated a moment, drew a deep breath that created a gentle ripple, and bent her leg so that the rounded curve of her knee peeked out of the water.

"She died in a car accident."

Adam watched her carefully for signs of withdrawal. When none came, he urged her with his silence to continue.

"Mama was much younger than Dad. She was twenty-five and he was forty when he married her. Before he met her, he'd never had time for a wife, he'd told everyone. He was married to Shady Point. The resort demanded all of his energy. But then one summer Mama came to the lodge. She was an artist from New York. She'd fallen in love with the lake from some articles she'd read and decided she wanted to spend time painting here. And when she arrived—"

Her faraway smile led Adam to conclude, "She fell in love with your father too."

She nodded. "She'd only intended to stay a month. Somehow, she never got around to leaving. They married right away and as Daddy used to joke, 'Nine months and fifteen minutes after the ceremony' I was born."

"They didn't waste any time."

She smiled again. "Not a minute."

They were both silent for a while, both thoughtful. "The day Mama died she was on her way home from International Falls. She'd gone to town to do some shopping. On the trip home a semi went out of control and hit her head-on."

Adam caressed the milky white knee that rose above the water.

"I was in bed when Daddy came to tell me. It was very dark and very quiet when he woke me up. Even now, I can remember how the room looked shaded in late-night shadows, the light spilling across my bed from the doorway. It's amazing how sleep can insulate. He was crying and I remember thinking, Daddy's playing a joke on me. You know, like parents do sometimes to little kids when they pretend to be sad because you wouldn't share your sucker, or some silly thing. And I remember thinking, I'm thirteen years old, not a little kid to play this silly game with . . . Anyway." The catch in her voice brought an unaccountable tightness to his chest. "He was crying and it didn't seem real. He lay down beside me and gathered me in his arms and told me Mama was dead. That she wouldn't ever be coming home again. 'Baby,' he said against my hair, 'I don't think I can live without her.'"

Adam drew in a shaky breath. "He loved her very much."

"Yes," she whispered, and skimmed her hand idly across the water. "Very much. He never recovered from losing her."

"And then he left you too."

Adam closed his eyes for a long moment. John had loved his wife too much to go on. He'd turned to the bottle and left Joanna to handle the loss all alone. It was no wonder she was so tough. She'd learned early to take it on the chin.

Poor little girl, he thought, and without a word, helped her out of the tub. He wrapped her carefully in a flannel blanket and carried her to the chair in front of the fire. His lips pressed to her hair, he held her close against his body and rocked her like a child.

Eight

Adam gave Jo pieces of himself a little at a time after that. At first the revelations came in unguarded moments, often as a response to something she'd said or done. The words slipped out with an ease he didn't stop to question. He merely let go. For the first time in his life, he let escape what he'd fought to keep locked inside. Sharing himself with her seemed as natural as breathing.

After breakfast, he helped her dress and, loaning her his sweatshirt, they headed outside.

In any season, Lake Kabetogama possessed a beauty that was a celebration of the magnificence of nature and a joy to all five senses. This particular day, the sun heralded the glory of autumn. It rimmed the treetops with gold and silvered the lake with its shimmering reflection. The aroma of evergreen and the pungent, musky scent of decaying leaves perfumed the crisp air.

The lake breeze was gentle. It wove a rustling, musical sound as it filtered through the forest, persuading the birch leaves to ride to the island floor in its wake. Feathering lazily to the ground, the golden discs decorated the rocky path they walked to the shore.

It was a day bathed in the same kind of magic that had blanketed their night. The illusion continued. Cocooned in the knowledge that until someone found them, they were lost to the rest of the world, they made the most of the brief suspension of time. They ignored the impending return of reality and found a sweet healing in each other.

Determined to make the best of the sunshine and the still water, Jo, with Adam's help, scavenged around in the toolshed and came up with some fishing gear. Although the pole had seen better days, she declared it to be serviceable. After a little more digging she found enough tackle to rig the line.

With more persuasion than she thought necessary, she playfully goaded Adam into trying his luck at fishing for their supper.

"Just think," she said brightly, "tonight we won't have to be subjected to another meal of dehydrated something-or-other that passes as real food."

After they'd settled down on a prominent rock ledge overlooking the bay, Adam reluctantly confessed he didn't have the slightest inkling of what to do.

"What do you expect from a street kid from Detroit?" he grumbled good-naturedly. "Why don't *you* do it?"

She waved her bandaged hand. "It's a two-handed sport, sport. Besides, I think I'm going to enjoy playing the part of teacher for a change."

The reminder of the kind of tutoring Adam had given her the previous night and then again that morning flooded her cheeks with crimson.

He pulled her up against him and kissed her hard. "Lord, you look pretty in pink."

"Quit trying to distract me." She laughed, squirming out of his arms, then patiently instructed him on the proper way to cast.

His huge hands, usually artful and articulate, became clumsy and unsure as he battled the intricacies of the rod and reel.

"I'm suddenly seeing the term 'all thumbs' in a new light," she said, teasing him about his botched attempt to cast into deeper water.

"You know," he drawled, arching a brow in warning, "I could throw *you* out there with a lot less difficulty than this line. I might enjoy it more, too, little girl, so don't push."

Taking pity on his frustration, she encouraged him gently. "It just takes practice. It's all wrist action and finesse."

"So ask me to finesse a wallet out of some mark's pocket, or the hubcaps from a car parked under a streetlight. I've had plenty of practice at both."

"I knew you had a shady past."

He laughed. "The shadiest. But just so your little heart doesn't go all a twitter, you couldn't be in safer hands than mine."

"I've always known that, too," she said, then added hesitantly, "but you do have my curiosity piqued. What is it you do in Detroit?"

He sobered as reality crept in. "I'm a cop."

She looked out over the bay. "A cop," she repeated, as if everything had just fallen into place.

"You sound surprised."

"No. Intrigued would be a better word. And it definitely explains a few things."

"Like?"

"Like that angry scar on your thigh. You were shot, weren't you? And you've got, in your words, 'time on your hands' because you're still healing." Concern darkened her eyes.

He looked away, knowing she deserved to hear the whole story but unable to find it in himself to relive it. She must have sensed the difficulty he was having, because she quickly steered clear of the subject.

"So you went from picking pockets and stealing hubcaps to one of Detroit's finest. What kind of a police force has a petty thief on its payroll?"

He gave her a slow, crooked grin. "A desperate one."

"You haven't really done those things, have you?"

"Those and a helluva lot worse. What you see before you is a product of a less than sterling upbringing. I was hustling for a buck before I was old enough to know that what I was doing was wrong. And I was damn good at it," he added, smiling ruefully. "I reached the ripe old age of twelve before I ever got caught."

"And that was the end of it?"

He grunted. "Just the beginning. I wore my little stint with juvenile probation like a medal and went right back out on the streets. By that time I was enjoying what I did, the thrill and all, the bucking of a society that didn't give a damn about me and my kind. And by then I'd sort of gotten used to eating."

"Where were your parents?" she asked so hesitantly, he suspected she'd already guessed the answer.

His jaw hardened for a moment, then he shrugged. "I never knew who my father was. My mother found herself pregnant at fifteen. She never tired of reminding me she'd given up her youth to raise me. We lived from one welfare check and allotment of commodities to the next. And whatever else I could scare up for rent money. Evidently, it finally got to be too much for her, because I came home one night and she was gone."

"Gone?"

"Split. She'd brought some drifter to the housing project about a week before. He must have promised greener pastures because . . . Hey, what's this?" Reaching out, he brushed away a single tear that tracked down her cheek. "Ah, Jo . . ."

Drawing her onto his lap he held her close. No one had ever cried for Adam Dursky. *Because* of him maybe, but never for him. Yet this tough little woman who refused to cry for herself, was crying for him. "Not for me, Jo. Don't cry for me. I was one of the lucky ones."

She nestled closer to his chest. "How so?"

"I found Jack Claypool. Or rather, he found me. Jack was a beat cop the summer I turned eighteen. One steamy July night he caught me trying to hot-wire a '67 Chevy."

She felt his chuckle against her cheek. "That's funny?"

"Jack *angry*, is funny. He's like an old bull seeing red. Anyway, he could have really nailed me, booked me as an adult. But he let me off with some fast talk and some honest caring. The man turned my life around. He got me into the marines and as the saying goes, 'it made a man out of me.'"

"You were in Vietnam." She reached shyly inside his shirt and ran her fingers along the long, shiny scar that hugged his rib cage. "Is that where you got this?" By now she knew the scar intimately, it and the one low on his groin, dangerously close to that part of him that responded to her slightest touch.

He gave her another kind of response now, a subtle tensing of his body. When his answer didn't immediately come, she pulled back, smiling an "it's okay" smile. "I shouldn't have asked."

Adam was stunned by her gesture. Before he could tell her it was all right, that he was ready to talk about it, a whirring sound sliced into the silence.

"Ohmygosh!" She jumped up off his lap and lunged for the fishing pole, barely catching it before it disappeared into the lake. "Adam, you've got one!" she cried, shoving the pole into his hand. "Don't sit there. Catch it!"

Watching her lose her cool had a calming effect on him. And she was something to watch, shouting heated instructions, her hair flying with frenzied activity around her face. Her excitement was infectious, though, and finally, despite her harried orders and his own ineptness, he landed the fish.

It was only by sheer luck that the aged monofilament line didn't snap against the weight of a nice-sized walleye.

"Oh, Adam," she cried, bubbling over with delight. "It's a beauty! And wait until you taste it."

Trying hard to hide his pride and wondering why a stupid thing like catching her a fish for her supper made him feel so full inside, he swung her, fish and all, into his arms.

"You'd by God better not burn it," he said as he stalked toward the cabin.

"Me? Oh, no." She laughed, wrapping her arms around his neck. "You catch 'em. You clean 'em. *You* cook 'em. It's the law of the wilderness."

He grunted and hefted her higher against his chest. "I think you've forgotten who the law really is in these parts, Red. Let's hope you get your attitude adjusted by the time we get back to the cabin."

Many hours later, with his stomach and his arms full, Adam looked down in utter contentment at the woman lying by his side. "I can't believe I let you talk me into this. It's freezing out here."

"But look at the sky . . . and wait. The show should start anytime now."

They were lying in a clearing under the stars, nestled together inside the sleeping bag like two squirming puppies. After eating their fill of fish, she'd done a little mental calculating and realized this was a night she'd been waiting for since the beginning of the summer. With some gentle coaxing, she'd convinced him he didn't want to miss what the night had in store.

Wrapping her tighter against him, he smoothed back the riot of red-gold curls and tucked her head beneath his chin. He felt her smile as she settled against him.

"Have you ever seen anything like it?" she asked after a while, looking up at the star-spackled sky. "The black is so black, the starlight so pure."

Her whispered sigh seemed not an intrusion on the quiet, but an integral part of the peaceful night. Without stopping to measure his thoughts for censure, he stared into the heavens and spoke. "I remember a night a lifetime ago when I lay under a midnight-black sky like this one. We were dug in at the edge of a rain forest waiting for morning and the Vietcong's next assault.

"And I remember wondering then, how could anything that beautiful be a part of a war so ugly?"

For a moment he was back there in the foxhole at the jungle's edge. The fear he'd felt as a nineteen-year-old soldier thousands of miles away from anything that was familiar colored his voice. "Hell, I was a city kid. I'd never seen a night sky without a layer of smog and manufactured light to dim its shine. I'd never seen a night so black. And I'd never been so scared. I was twenty-one days away from going stateside and I hadn't received so much as a scratch. And deep inside, I knew they'd never let me go home that way . . ."

He felt her heartbeat accelerate against his chest and drew her closer. "We'd held repeated fronts. Our casualties had been heavy. The constant barrage from snipers and the remoteness of our location had whittled us down to a small, scraggly platoon of scared kids and crazy men. Rations and ammunition were low. Morale was nonexistent.

"Just before morning light, they came. Hundreds of them. Screaming like banshees, swarming like flies."

In spite of the cool night air, beads of sweat broke out on his forehead. "I'm still not sure why I'm alive. Probably because they thought they'd killed me. I'd emptied my rifle on the first wave and was trying to reload when the magazine jammed. The first Cong over the rim of the foxhole made a wild jab with his bayonet, then clubbed me with the butt of his rifle.

"The next thing I remember, I was on a gurney in an EVAC unit near Da Nang with a hell of a headache and a hole the size of Michigan in my gut. And I was one of the lucky ones . . ."

He drew a shuddering breath, remembering the sounds and stench of the dying and the dead. He'd never spoken to anyone about his memories of the killing and the atrocities of war. Not even Annie. Reliving them was as painful as bleeding. The hurt would go on for as long as he lived. Yet as he closed his eyes against the horror, he found that with the telling, something had changed. Somehow, the memories were less vivid, a bit more distant. He relaxed and let the images roll through his mind and out of his subconscious like a vintage newsreel.

Jo's silence was more supportive than words, her presence more potent than drink. And drinking was all he'd wanted to do after he'd come back to the states. He'd done a lot of things he'd been sorry for. Yet as he lay in the arms of this small, giving woman, a peace settled over him and a feeling of freedom from that part of his past. He felt a strong sense of communion with her and, surprisingly, more in touch with himself than he'd been in too many years.

When she wrapped her arms tighter around him, he realized how long he'd been silent. She ran her hand back and forth along the scar on his side, then lower. "Do they still hurt you?" she asked with an ingenuousness only someone as pure as Joanna could have.

"No. There's no pain, but . . ."

"But?" she urged when he hesitated.

"But the general consensus is that the infection did its damage."

She tipped her face to his. He brushed the hair back from her forehead and answered her questioning frown. "Lord, girl, haven't you wondered? As many times as we've made love, we've never used protection." He heard the hollow emptiness in his tone. "I'll never father children, Joanna. Did you think I'd risk the possibility of a pregnancy knowing that when I left, you'd be forced to deal with it alone?"

Jo couldn't say what hurt her more. The fact that he'd voiced the inevitability of his leaving, or his unspoken pain over the loss he'd suffered. And no, she hadn't wondered. She'd just accepted what they'd shared and not once considered the potential consequences.

"I'm sorry," she whispered, and dropped her head to his chest again. "You should have been a father. You'd have made a good one."

A thousand splintering emotions ricocheted through him. He wanted to hold her forever, to absorb the healing balm of her spirit and reconstruct the shambles his life had become. He'd never felt more whole as when he was with this woman. And he'd never felt as bleak as when he faced the prospect of life without her.

"Adam!" Her excited whisper brought him back to the night. "Look. It's starting."

A brilliant streak of white light arched across the indigo sky. It was followed by another, then a profusion of rocketing fireballs trailed by diamond-dusted tails. The shooting stars criss-crossed and careened through the heavens like fireworks on the Fourth of July. The meteor shower was as stunning and as brilliant as she had promised.

"Have you ever seen anything as beautiful?" she asked with breathless awe.

His dark gaze lowered to her face. The star glow reflected in her eyes showed the wonder with which she watched the sky. "I hadn't . . . until I met you."

He loved her slowly that night, with exquisite awareness of her pleasure, with torturous knowledge that when he left he would cause her pain. Their days together might be numbered, but he intended to do everything in his power to make the most of them.

She evidently had the same idea.

"Come on," she said playfully as she knelt beside him the next morning, extending a cup of coffee for them to share. "It's a beautiful day. Let's explore the island."

He yawned and braced himself on his elbows to look at her. She was all bright green eyes and challenging smiles as he leaned toward her morning kiss.

Loving this joyful side of her, he followed her lead. "I can save you the trouble, Red," he said, teasing her with a lazy smile. "To your left is rock, water, and pine. To your right is rock, water, and birch." He paused for a careful swallow of hot coffee. "And to your immediate front and center is a man who's too tired to do anything but look at you."

She considered his sleepy speech, grinning mischievously. "What do you suppose it would take to put a little life into those old bones?" she asked, toying with the top button of her shirt.

"Oh, no." He sat up laughing, when the first button slipped free of the buttonhole. "Any more of *that* kind of exercise and they'll be feeding me intravenously for a month."

Her staged attempt to look put out broadened his smile. The self-effacing, sexually shy girl who'd come to him that first night would never have had the confidence to engage in this kind of love play. This woman had reached fulfillment. He felt a sudden stirring of response to the invitation from his wild, uninhibited lover.

"All right then," she countered, trying another tack, "what about the prospect of a little excitement?"

"I repeat," he said, intentionally misunderstanding, "any more of that kind of exercise—"

Her bubbly laughter cut him off. "I was thinking more along the lines of mystery and intrigue."

He eyed her suspiciously over the rim of the cup. "On Jug Island?"

"Especially on Jug Island. Surely you've wondered how Jug got its name."

"I've wondered how I ended up here, I've wondered how you ever survived long enough to get here . . . and I've wondered about that little mole on the inside of your left thigh." He grinned, thoroughly enjoying her blush. "But to tell you the honest truth, Red, I've never wondered how Jug got its name. Should I have?"

"Absolutely. Local legend has it that Jug has a history of illicit goings-on."

He was fully awake now and his wicked grin

suggested he might be interested—at least in the illicit part. Propping his arm on an updrawn knee, he handed her the coffee. "Such as?" he asked, playing with a strand of the red hair he seemed always compelled to touch.

"Such as moonshine and prohibition booze."

He arched a brow. "In Minnesota?"

"Of course in Minnesota, and specifically here. Remember, we're only minutes away from the Canadian border by boat. Kabetogama runs into Lake Namakan and Namakan is in Canada. It was a short dash across the border with the illegal hooch. Jug and the way the mouth of Blue Fin Bay is practically hidden unless you're looking for it, made the perfect place to stash the goods."

"Stash the goods? Illegal hooch?" He tugged her onto his lap. "You watch a lot of old Bogart movies up here in the winter, Red?"

"Go ahead, make fun of me. But I happen to know that Capone himself once walked Jug's shores."

"Looking for his stash, no doubt." He wiggled his eyebrows Groucho Marx style, then pulled an appropriately serious face to match her scowl. "All right. I'm sorry. Tell me more. What brought Capone to Jug Island?"

"He came to check out the location for a possible drop."

"Oh." He nodded sagely. "He was casing the joint, huh?"

Her eyes narrowed and her chin came up a notch. "You have an incredibly smart mouth for a man with a bad leg and a cup of steaming hot coffee balanced over his lap."

He threw back his head and laughed. "And you've got a hell of a lot of cheek for such a little girl," he said, hugging her tight. "No . . . no . . . not the coffee. I'll be good, I promise. Please . . . do continue."

Over a breakfast of leftover fish, she convinced him with animated gestures, wide-eyed excitement, and suspiciously sincere accounts that Jug had in fact been a drop point for contraband liquor during the Roaring Twenties.

"Somewhere on the island," she said, "though no one knows for sure where, there is said to be a cave. And in the cave is an undelivered shipment of bootleg booze, still fermenting in its stone 'jugs.'"

"Hence the name Jug Island?" he concluded, now mildly curious. He regarded her thoughtfully, a fork full of fish poised over his plate. "There's more to the story, right?"

She nodded and got up to refill their coffee cups. "There's supposed to be money in the cave, Capone's money, gold bullion, left for safekeeping until he could come back for it."

"I can't believe no one's found the cave by now. From what I've seen of the island, it's not all that big."

"True, but there're so many ravines and crevices in the rock that if the bootleggers were clever, they could have easily hidden the entrance. Over the years, the undergrowth could have erased any evidence of the cave's existence."

"And you think we can find it today?"

She shrugged, rounded the table, and settled herself down on his lap. "We could give it a try." She smiled demurely and tried some trick with her eyelashes. "Unless you can think of something better to do."

He shook his head sadly. "You were such a *nice* little girl when I met you." He kissed her soundly and lifted her off his lap. "And yes, I can think of a hundred things I'd *rather* do. But my body is forbidding me to even entertain such thoughts . . . for now." He punctuated his warning with a leering grin, then rose, grabbed his jacket from the peg by the door, and tossed her his sweatshirt. "Last one to the cave is a 'dirty rat,' see?"

"*Who's* been watching old movies?" she asked archly, and nestled into the spot he made for her under his arm as they squeezed out the door.

They didn't find the gold. They didn't even find the cave. And it was only after Adam's good-natured grumblings about his suspicions she'd been talking through her hat that she admitted she may have stretched the truth just a bit. But only the part about Capone . . . and about the gold . . . and maybe about the bootleg brew. She *did* know that a man named Jensen used to keep his "jug" of moonshine hidden out here from his wife, and wasn't it nice that Adam had gotten some exercise after all?

Then she'd run like hell when he came roaring after her like a thwarted mobster.

No, they didn't find the gold, but they did find a sun-drenched glen. Sheltered from the wind by a coppice of cedar and pine, softened by island grass and moss, their island bed was warm and secluded. Their lovemaking was lusty and lush. Only the eagle, gliding in the blue sky above them, soared higher.

Nine

Jo lay sprawled across Adam's pounding chest, their hearts hammering in tandem as they languished in a gradual meltdown of spent desire. His hands were tangled in her hair, his breath slow and heavy against the top of her head. Replete and relaxed, she let herself drift on the currents of deep satisfaction.

The sun felt warm against her bare skin; the southerly breeze was a friendly caress. Adam was solid and strong beneath her. Her question was completely unexpected.

"Have you ever been married?"

It surprised them both, disrupting the moment, jangling into the present like the distant rumble of an oncoming train.

His hands knotted tighter in her hair, and he pressed her closer to his body. In the long moment before he spoke, both wondered how much he would disclose.

"Are you sure you want to hear this?"

"Only if you want to tell me."

She felt his chest constrict, then relax under her cheek.

"When they shipped me home from 'Nam, it was to a VA hospital in Virginia to recover."

Her hand moved reflexively across his scar. "How long were you there?"

"Too long. Several months. It wasn't so much the bayonet wounds and the concussion as it was the infection that kept me down. What blood I had left when they dug me out of that foxhole was full of poison. I lay there for over forty-eight hours before the cleanup crew came in and found me."

Adam didn't tell her they'd thought he was dead. He'd been dragged out of the pile of bodies in that bloody hole and only his unconscious moan had saved him from a body bag. Yet she shivered, as if piecing together the rest of the picture herself. Reaching above his head, he found the sweatshirt and covered her with it to keep away the chill.

She snuggled closer to his warmth.

"Anyway, it was in the hospital that I met Annie. She was a volunteer on my ward."

The silence stretched between them. Each for their own reasons was hesitant for him to continue. He began again slowly, measuring his words. "Annie was everything my life had never been. She was kind, caring, and obviously vulnerable. I was a 'wounded warrior' and she empathized. She must have thought she saw something in me—I don't know what—that made her think she loved me. It wasn't long after my release that she convinced me we should get married."

Now that he'd started, Jo wasn't sure she wanted to hear the rest of it. Yet she sensed it was as important for him to tell her as it was for her to know.

"Jack had a spot waiting for me on the police force and when no other prospects turned up, I felt I had to take it."

"It wasn't what you wanted to do?"

"I didn't know what I wanted to do. I was broke, I needed a job, and I'd come back to a country that didn't seem to give a damn that I'd killed in its name . . . that I'd damn near been killed. In short, nothing had changed."

"Except you had Annie."

He stared at the awning of blue sky, deciding the vastness above him equaled the magnitude of his transgressions. "Except I had Annie. Annie and Jack. They were the most important things in the world to me. I owed Jack, so I took the job and adjusted. Annie never did. She was too gentle, too fragile. She couldn't adapt to life as a vice cop's wife. And then, too, she wanted something I couldn't give her. Children. After seven years of marriage, it had become apparent that the marine doctor's speculation about my being sterile was actually fact.

"And then," he said after a long pause, "there was the drinking."

Unaware, he ran his hand up and down the length of her back, pressing her closer against him with each long sweeping caress. "She never knew if I was going to show up drunk or sober. Neither did I. One night I came home pretty badly beaten up after a particularly nasty bust. Annie was horrified. She issued an ultimatum. Either I leave the force or she'd leave me. Said she didn't want to sit by and watch me systematically destroy myself, whether it was with booze or for the good of the department."

"What happened?"

His hand stopped midmotion. "I called her bluff. I didn't feel I had a choice. I guess she didn't either. She wanted out, so she left. And I let her go."

"You loved her," Jo said very softly.

"Yes."

"And now?" Her voice was softer still.

"And now . . ." His tired sigh stretched into an eternity. "And now it doesn't matter. What happened between Annie and me was a long time ago, fifteen years. I'm not the same man I was then. Hell, I'm not the same man I was two months ago. I'm not sure I want to be . . . I'm not even sure anymore if I can be."

Jo levered her weight above him with her good hand. The unqualified love he saw in her eyes made his chest constrict with emotion.

"I don't know what you were," she said, "but I think I know what you are now."

He shook his head. The self-disgust that had been quietly festering inside him erupted unexpectedly as anger—at himself for revealing so much of his life, at her for her unwavering trust. Trust he hadn't earned and didn't deserve.

"No," he said defeatedly. Gripping her by the shoulders, he held her away. "You know nothing of what I am. Nothing."

"Then tell me." Her eyes issued a challenge he wasn't ready to face. "Tell me what you think I don't already know."

In clench-jawed silence, he set her away from him. Rising stiffly, he jerked on his jeans. She followed his lead, quietly dressing, waiting for him to vent the anger that had slammed between them like a wedge.

Without a word, he tugged the fly of her jeans together, snapped and zipped them shut. The silence became poignant with the implications of his tender attention, then brittle with his unspoken tension as he knelt and tied her shoes.

The silence held as they began walking through the forest toward the cabin. The wind rustled through the pines. Its breezy song was a melody Jo had grown up with. Once foreign to Adam's ears, its whisper was now intrinsically meshed in his conscious. Its gentle caress stole the last of his anger and brought home the fact that needed facing. She was in love with him. That certain knowledge filled him with awe . . . and bludgeoned him with guilt. If he did one decent, honest deed in his life, it would be to convince her he wasn't worthy. She was a woman full of passion. She needed a man to share it with—a whole man.

He stooped to snag a fallen piece of birch bark and systematically shredded the paper-thin parchment as they walked. For the past few days he'd let loose pieces of his past. The one piece that mattered remained untold. It was time she knew about the man he really was.

"Frank Keller had been my partner for fifteen of the twenty years I'd been on the force," he said without preamble. "Not once in all that time did he let me down. Not once did he leave me vulnerable. I was his backup the night he was shot. Because I screwed up, Sharon Keller goes to bed alone every night and is now trying to eke a living out of a police widow's pension. That's what you need to know about me, Red. Now maybe you can believe what I've been trying to tell you. I'm not a man you can depend on."

She was quiet for a time, and when she finally spoke, her voice was reedy with the strain of uncertainty. "I've never been where you've been, Adam, so I can't begin to relate to what happened. But I think I know you well enough to realize that your partner's death couldn't have been your fault. You're too much of a protector. You put too much into what you do."

She seemed to come to a conclusion then. "That's the reason you ended up here, isn't it? You needed some time off to deal with what happened to him. Boy, what a sorry waste of your time."

"What are you talking about?"

"Instead of helping me, you should have been

coming to terms with what happened, owning up to the truth that you weren't responsible."

"I *am* responsible."

"No. You're not. And you need to let the guilt go."

"Just cut it loose like a fish that's too small to keep?" he bit out.

"Yes," she answered emphatically, reacting to the sarcasm in his voice. "Just cut it loose. Holding on isn't going to bring your partner back. You're fighting something you can't defeat and until you recognize that, you'll never be able to get on with your life."

"Lord, if it were only that simple."

"It *is* that simple," she insisted softly.

"Just like it's so simple for you to forgive your father for leaving you, and to forgive yourself. You talk a good line, but you don't fool me, Joanna. You still blame yourself for his leaving, just like you did when you were a child. You blame yourself for driving him away."

Her eyes revealed her hurt and the fact that he'd hit upon the truth. Still, he persisted. "But there's the difference between us. You're wrong to bear the blame. In my case, I'm the only one who *can* bear it."

As usual, she brushed over her own hurts to help with his. "I won't pretend to know what you were up against, but no matter how vehemently you deny it, I *do* know you. I know what kind of man you are. You've shown me with your actions. You've told me with your care. And I know the truth when I see it. I've no doubt that every time you went out on the streets you took the same risks your partner did. It could have been you, not him."

"No it couldn't! I screwed up and because of it, he's dead."

She stopped him with a hand on his arm.

"Convince me you're as guilty as you feel you need to be." The look in her eyes was gentle but demanding. "Tell me what happened."

He glowered at her. "You want the thumbnail sketch, or all the gory details?" he asked bitterly, then made the decision for her.

Talking to himself as much as to her, he resumed his slow gait up the path. "The Oldtown merchants had been experiencing a multitude of break-ins. We got a lead on who was responsible. It was a street gang that had been rumored to be behind a number of thefts and beatings in that end of town. We'd been looking for something concrete to pin on those thugs for months. Finally, we got a solid tip and set up a stakeout we hoped would put an end to the terrorism."

He stopped walking and looked hard at some unseen spot in the forest, rethinking the series of events as they'd transpired. He shook his head helplessly. "It should have been routine. Frank was covering the front of the liquor store and I was at the back waiting for it all to come down. When I heard shots, I broke through the back door. Frank had one of them spread-eagled against a counter. I checked his back just as this—" He broke off, choking on the memory. "—just as this kid came up behind him. I recognized him. It was Juan Gomez. He was a kid from the projects. I'd been working out with him at the gym. I couldn't believe it was Juan, didn't *want* to believe it. That split second of indecision was all the time he needed to shoot Frank and turn his gun on me. Frank was dead and I was down with a bullet in my thigh before I ever got a shot off."

He cupped the back of his neck with one hand and stood quietly, willing the thundering in his chest to ease the pain that was always with him.

"He was fifteen years old. Fifteen years old! He killed my partner and crippled me. Once I started firing I didn't stop until I'd emptied the clip." He breathed an oath through clenched teeth, wishing he had a wall to shove his fist through. "I saw so much of myself in the boy. I wanted to be for him what Jack had been for me. I wanted to give him a chance. He'd been a hard case but he was beginning to come around, you know?"

His eyes burned into hers with the torment of a thousand questions and as many sins. "How do I justify what I've done? How do I tuck that little bit of history away in the back of my mind and say, hey, it wasn't my fault? How do I live with killing a child and with leaving a good woman a widow? And where, for God's sake, do I find the courage to go back on those streets again?"

His questions were addressed to her, but asked of himself. He'd been searching for the answers for over two months. "I lost more than my partner that night. I lost my nerve."

He turned to her, his expression hardened by rage. "So wipe the stars out of your eyes and the hero worship out of your mind, Red. What you see before you is just an old, used-up man. A used-up cop. A coward. I break out in a cold sweat just thinking about facing a dark alley alone, about the next punk waiting in the shadows with a switchblade or a gun. There's nothing, *nothing* I want to do less than go back there. And some nights, there's nothing I want more than a drink of liquid courage." He turned away, staring out into space again.

"You know," he went on reflectively after a minute, "you hit the nail dead center that day when you asked me if I was running from some kind of trouble. You were right, in capital letters. I told myself I wasn't, but I *was* running. I *am* running. I'm scared down to my socks to go back to Detroit."

"But you'll go."

He shook his head, looking to the sky for relief. "I'll go . . . because worthless as my miserable life is, I have to live it. I have to look at this face in the mirror every morning. I have to learn to deal with what I did. And I have to face those streets again or I'll never have a moment's peace the rest of my life."

"And where will you find your peace, Adam?" she asked him carefully. "In the layers of guilt you wrap around yourself like an indictment? Will your self-blame bring Frank or the boy back? Do you honestly think you are so exclusively liable that you can take responsibility for lives other than your own?"

She frowned at him thoughtfully. "Frank knew the risks he took the same as you did. And the boy could have gained by his association with you. It was his choice not to, just as it was yours all those years ago to accept the hand Jack offered you. Just as the choice is yours now to accept that you were *not* your partner's keeper, or the boy's. You were not to blame. You're not a coward. You're a strong, honest man."

He whirled on her, his eyes stormy. All the anguish and anger of his past failures got mixed up with the wrongs he'd done to this woman. "Strong? Honest?" he lashed out. He had to convince her he wasn't worth losing sleep over, had to convince himself to leave her while the thought of doing just that boiled like an infection in his blood. "You're deceiving yourself, Joanna, if you see those things in me. Was I strong where you were concerned? Was I honest when I told myself it wouldn't hurt you when I left?"

"Oh, no." She shook her head vehemently. "No you don't. You're not going to add me to your list of transgressions. I don't belong there."

"I *am* going to leave you. You know that, don't you?"

Silence fell between them, weighted with layers of anger and regret and doubt.

"So who's asking you to stay?" she challenged tightly, her pride showing.

She stalked away from him, hugging her arms around her middle. "You know what your problem is, Dursky?" she threw back over her shoulder. She stopped and rounded on him, filled with pain and fury. "You're no different from any other man in this male-dominated, macho-intellect society you've helped to create. You're never going to accept the fact that you do not have the power to carry the weight of the world on your shoulders, broad as they may be. You are not responsible for the condition of a society that breeds the violence in the streets of Detroit, or any other city. You can't move mountains and you can't make all wrongs into rights."

She drew herself up a little straighter. Unintimidated by his scowl, she squared her shoulders. "And you don't have the market cornered on every sin or weakness known to mankind. Hasn't it ever occurred to you that the rest of us aren't perfect either? My demons may not be as big and bad as yours, but I've got them just the same. You aren't the only one hiding out. I'm hiding, too, behind a comfortable little dream that I needed to come home to rebuild Shady Point. You want to know the whole truth?" she asked angrily, raking the hair back out of her eyes. "I thought maybe, just maybe, if I could make things the way they used to be, my father might love me enough to come home.

"So you see," she continued, ignoring his surprised expression, "you aren't alone in your weakness. And you are *not* responsible for me. I will not live and die by your good graces. I know my own mind. I knew exactly what I was getting myself into when I took you to my bed. And you'd do well to remember that. *I* took *you* to *my* bed. You didn't take me to yours. It was my decision. My choice. And I'll be damned if I'll let you shoulder the responsibility for what happened between us. If I hadn't wanted it to happen, it wouldn't have. And if I wanted you to stay, I'd ask you to."

Her eyes flared with fiery pride as she leveled her parting shot. "So you can leave here with a clear conscience, Dursky. You'll have to look a little harder for an excuse to pummel yourself with another fistful of blame for all your fabricated transgressions. I refuse to give you even a thimbleful of guilt to add to your overflowing cup. The only thing you've done to hurt me is to demean what we've shared by infusing it with that guilt." Tears burned her eyes. She fought them and met his hard stare with her head held high. "But I'm a big girl and I can handle it. And as I believe I've already mentioned, I can take care of myself." She whirled away, leaving him staring after her.

Adam didn't follow her into the cabin. He grabbed the axe and headed for the woodpile.

An hour later, the pain in his back almost overshadowed the ache in his gut. He tossed the last split log on the pile, then mopped the sweat from his face and neck with the shirt he'd discarded.

He loved her, dammit. Her spirit, her anger, her trust.

She needed a young man who could share her vision and her burdens, not an old one whose confidence was shattered and would be a burden himself. She needed a man to give her babies and enhance her life, not a sterile cynic who would wallow in the injustices life had dealt him and drag her down because of them.

Swearing, he sank the double-edged blade into

the chopping block with a resounding thwack. Her fiery speech hadn't fooled him. She accepted the fact that he had to go and was trying to make it easy for him by driving a distance between them as sharply as he drove the steel into the dry cedar. The very least he could do was help her make the break by staying the hell away from her.

The shadows had lenghtened and melded into darkness by the time he turned to the cabin. A dim light flickered in the window. He watched it for an eternity, longing for something that could not be, before he shrugged into his shirt. Not bothering with the buttons, he gathered an armful of wood against his chest, ignoring the bite of the cleanly cut edges that creased his bare skin.

He climbed the stairs slowly. With each step he resolved to hold at bay the need to take her into his arms and love her until right and wrong ceased to matter. But when he opened the door he was enfolded in the warm fire she'd kindled, and by the invitation in her eyes. All was forgiven.

"Come over by the fire where it's warm," she said.

He stood very still, his arms full of wood, his chest full of want, amazed by her capacity for giving.

She was standing by the hearth, bewitching and beautiful, dressed in nothing but the fragrance of her just-washed skin, and her old flannel shirt.

Dragging his gaze away from her, he crossed the room to drop the wood in the woodbox. He brushed his palms on his thighs, lost the battle, and turned to her. She raised her unbandaged hand to push the hair back from her eyes. The unbuttoned placket of the shirt fell open. He clenched his jaw and feasted on the pale, supple flesh exposed beneath it.

She made no pretense as to how she wanted the remaining time between them to be shared. "Not everyone is granted this gift we've been given," she said. "We've known from the onset this time was special, and temporary. I accept it. Let's not waste another minute on regrets and recriminations." She took a step toward him and held out her arms. "Come love me, Adam."

How two people, in such a short span of time, could reach so many impasses was a mystery to him. With her blistering assessment of his self-image, she had denied him his guilt and shunned his regret. And now, she offered him her love. The tight fist of tension that had gripped his chest relaxed its hold as the fight left and his love for her entered.

"Just once," he whispered raggedly as he closed the distance between them, "I wish I could resist you."

She moved easily into his arms. "And just once," she said on a wistful sigh, "I wish I could have come to you in satin or silk." Her fingers skimmed the marks the wood had left across the warm skin of his chest.

He held her against him like a dying man embracing his last sunset. Threading his fingers through her hair, he cupped her head in his hands and tipped her face to his.

"You *are* satin . . ." he murmured against the curls at her temple. With trembling hands he brushed the flannel from her shoulders.

She stood naked before him. He went down on one knee and pressed his open mouth to her belly, moistening the velvety skin with his tongue. With a slow hungry caress, he committed to memory the slight curve of her hip, the gentle thrust of her upturned breasts, the tautness of her distended nipples. "You are silk . . ."

His accolade was a whisper against her tingling flesh as he gathered her in his arms and laid her down before the fire. "And you could come to me in sackcloth," he added as he lowered his mouth to the soft, warm part of her that pulsed with wanting and that he ached to fill, "as long as you come to me."

Always before this night, their lovemaking had been overshadowed for him by guilt, by regret, by the desperate knowledge that the same twist of fate that had brought them together would also break them apart. Because he now knew he loved her, because he knew that by leaving her he was giving her the chance to make a better life without him, the inevitable parting became less painful to contemplate.

He couldn't promise her forever, but he could give her the night. What he couldn't say with words, he said with touch. What he couldn't heal with apologies, he soothed with the reverent caress of his mouth. His lovemaking was at once gentle and intense. The fencing that had been a standard part of their love games was over. He took her to the limit and back again.

Her face was flushed from the stunning depths of his passion, her eyes still misted with ecstasy's tears as she bent over him. Her hair sheathed his thighs and chest, and he groaned as her untutored mouth and small, thrilling hands made the sweetest love he'd ever known.

The next morning, his scent was on her skin, mingling with her own delicious fragrance as she leaned over him to pour another cup of coffee. Her hair was wild, tangled. The beautiful damage had been done by his hands the night before and added to that morning. He thought he'd never get his fill of seeing her this way.

Their eyes met and held. "Come here, Joanna."

He held out his hand and led her to the rocker

before the fire, where she curled up on his lap and let him hold her.

The rocker creaked like the ticking of a clock as they watched the fire and let their thoughts drift.

"You asked me the other night how I got used to the solitude." Her voice was soft against his chest. "I've been thinking about what it must have been like for you, coming from the city. It must have been difficult. I'm used to long winters when the snow is so deep and it's so cold out that weeks go by and you never see another human soul."

"Where I came from when I arrived here," he said, "had less to do with geography than it did with state of mind. I'd already isolated myself from everything that had been important to me. I'd spent a month in the hospital healing from the gunshot, another month in my apartment licking my wounds and flirting with Jim Beam and making life a living hell for everyone in the precinct. They'd put me and my attitude behind a desk until I was 'fully recovered.' In my sergeant's words, when I wasn't chewing ass like a bear with a thorn in its paw, I was staring into space in a catatonic stupor." His chest expanded with his deep sigh. "In short, I was as useless to the department as I was to myself."

She ran her hand across his shoulder in a soothing caress. "He was a wise man to give you time to heal."

He laughed abruptly and hugged her tight. "When he cut me loose and I turned in my badge and gun, I'd never been so scared in my life. He was forcing me to face my demons alone. No work, no buffer of any kind between me and myself and my distant attraction to the bottle."

"Yet you let it alone."

"Yeah," he said, sounding a little surprised. "I did." He tucked her head under his chin and idly stroked her hair. Their unspoken thoughts ran parallel. They were thinking of John.

"He needs you, Jo. And if you'll stop and think about it, you need him too."

"He knows where to find me."

He sighed and rested his chin on the top of her head. "He could help take care of you if you'd let him."

"No one takes care of me, Dursky. You ought to know that by now."

"Remind me of that next time I tie your shoes." He felt her smile against his skin. "What will you do if you lose the lodge?"

She was quiet for a long moment, then she shrugged. "I had a good position in a relatively prestigious advertising agency in St. Paul. They told me when I left that they'd always have a spot for me. I don't know. Maybe I'll go back there. And maybe I'll take my shotgun to the auction and threaten anyone with a mind to bid against me."

She snuggled closer, savoring what she suspected would be some of her final moments with Adam. The lake had calmed dramatically during the past day. It wouldn't be long before someone, Steve probably, came looking for them.

She wouldn't cling, she promised herself. When the time came, she'd let him go. She'd let him leave with a clear conscience. She'd let him leave without saying the words, I love you.

Yet she knew without question that he did. In his absence, that knowledge would take the edge off the pain of living the rest of her life without him.

Quickly wiping a damning tear from her eye, she manufactured some innocuous question and was about to ask it, when she heard the roar of an approaching motorboat.

Their gazes collided. The closed look in his eyes said it all. She felt a sense of loss that was paralyzing. It was over. Reality had arrived.

Ten

Looking back, she felt like she'd lived an entire life span during those few days with Adam on Jug Island. Now, three months later, it all seemed a lifetime away. All but her memories. She held each one close, her heart twisting painfully as she recalled with crystal clarity the many times he had loved her.

He was gone. It was a fact she wrestled with daily.

She had more important things to worry about than missing him, though. She had bills to pay, the rest of the winter to get through. She wasn't complaining. That she was still at Shady Point, and that the threat of losing the lodge to the Dreamscape Corporation had never materialized, remained a miracle to her. When the day of the auction had arrived, she'd gone prepared to watch her hopes slip away. But the threatened bid never came. She'd left the auction stunned, elated, and wishing Adam were there to share her joy.

But he wasn't there. He never would be.

The day Steve had arrived at Jug, with a very lonesome Cooper practically mauling both her and Adam in greeting, Adam had packed his duffel and returned to Detroit.

Forcing herself to concentrate on her work, Jo picked up her pen and finished the edits on the new brochure she'd designed to advertise the lodge. She'd been working on the layout since one o'clock that afternoon. It was due at the printers after Christmas.

Christmas. She looked longingly across the room to the little tree she'd set up in the corner. Christmas was only a week away. Shoving aside the empty feeling that accompanied the thought of spending another holiday alone, she reviewed her edits.

Satisfied the brochure was to her liking, she rubbed at the stiffness in her neck and flicked on the lamp. It would be dark soon.

Rising slowly from the desk, she plugged in the tree lights, then walked to the frost-laced window that overlooked the lake. Mother Nature had perfected winter in northern Minnesota. Two feet of ice covered Kabetogama. Another twelve inches of pristine white snow topped the frozen lake like a thick layer of stiff frosting. Only the snowmobile tracks tracing across the shoreline marred the wind-sculpted skiffs. The beauty was both breathtaking and isolating.

She closed her eyes and pressed her forehead to the cold glass. She thought of spring. When the thaw began in early May, the lake would moan and cry as the cracking ice broke up and departed. The mournful sounds would echo hauntingly through the Northland, crying for winter's return much as she had cried for the return of her lover.

He wouldn't come back, but oh, how she missed him. As never before, she understood her father's pain.

She understood, too, Adam's need for a quick

departure. The break had been clean and final. The pain cut decisively deep.

A thunderous pounding on her door and Cooper, bolting up from his rug in front of the fire with a startled "Woof!" jolted her out of her reflections. Swiping a telling tear from her eye, she quieted the dog and hurried across the room to the door, wondering who would be out and about near dusk in this cold.

"Steve!"

"Crimanently it's cold out there," he announced unnecessarily as a zephyr of arctic wind zipped inside before he could slam the door shut behind him. Stomping the snow from his boots, he tugged off his gloves, then flipped back his fur-lined hood and unzipped his parka. His cheeks were mottled with red, his black hair matted and mussed as he shrugged out of his winter gear.

"Got a hot cup of coffee for a cold, thirsty man?" he asked with a shiver. He combed his hair with stiff fingers and walked over to the fireplace.

"What are you doing out on a day like this?" she asked. "They just announced on the radio that the windchill factor is sixty below and dropping."

He blew on his fingers to warm them, then scratched Cooper behind the ears. "It's good to see you too." His smile was saccharine sweet.

She brought him his coffee and a weak apology. "I'm sorry. It's just that I worry about you out in the cold."

"Maybe I worry about you too," he countered gently. "You shouldn't be alone here. Especially now."

She turned her back on him and walked over to the window again. "I'm fine."

"Sure you are . . . and I'm the abominable snowman. Talk to me. Convince me I shouldn't worry."

"What could possibly be wrong?" She whirled on

him, suddenly angry at him for knowing her too well, angrier at herself for confiding in him one long lonely night a month ago.

Uncharacteristic tears crowded against her lashes. Steve looked away, uncomfortable with her pain, and settled himself on her overstuffed sofa. He stared at the coffee cup dangling between his wide spread knees and sighed deeply. "The offer still stands, Jo."

She responded only with silence.

"I know you still love him," he added. "But I know you care about me too. There's enough, Jo. We've got more going for us than a lot of people begin or end a marriage with. We're friends. We could pull it off."

"Is that what you want for yourself? A buddy?" She shook her head and smiled sadly. They'd been through so much together. The summer Steve was twelve and he'd broken his leg, Jo had been driving the boat when he'd tried a dry landing on water skis, miscalculated, and hit the dock. She'd been the first to sign his cast. And when she'd lost her mother, Steve had been the one to brave her grief. The special bond that often breaks during the passage from the simplicities of childhood to the complexities of adulthood had remained intact between them.

And right now, as he sat there and offered to take care of her, she'd never loved him more. "I wouldn't do that to you. You're right. You *are* a good friend. And you deserve much more than what I've got to offer." When he searched her face too intensely, she squared her shoulders and smiled. "I'll be all right."

"It won't be easy."

"I can handle it."

"You'll at least let me help?"

She walked over to the sofa, sat down beside

him, and let him pull her into his arms. "I'll hold you to it."

He squeezed her hard. "Well." His voice sounded suspiciously gravelly as he let her go. "I'd best be on my way before it gets any darker. Have you got enough wood?"

She nodded.

"Phone working?"

"Yes, Mother. And I've got the CB if the lines go down. Don't worry. If I need you, I'll call."

He bundled up in silence, watching her all the while. "Jo . . . are you sure you're going to be okay?"

"Hey." She rallied for his benefit. "It's me, Ms. Independence, remember?"

He tugged her into his arms for a farewell hug. "Yeah, I remember. Take care, brat."

She grinned. "I love you too." Closing the door behind him, she listened until she could no longer hear the roar of his snowmobile.

The long shadows of dusk had darkened the house by the time she walked to the kitchen. She stared out the window and watched the sunset paint the snowy white lake a soft muted blue while she waited for her soup to heat. She wasn't hungry, but she ate anyway. She no longer had just herself to think about. She had the baby to consider.

Night brought the best and the worst times for Jo. She missed Adam most in the darkness. Because she missed him, she would let herself remember. And when she remembered, it made it all seem real and brought him back for a precious little while.

Each night as she lay alone beneath her cool, coarse sheets, she would press her hands to her belly and think of Adam's baby growing there. And she'd smile. Would it please him, this life they'd created with their love? Would it thrill him as it had her? She would never know, and neither would Adam. She would not have him coming back to her out of duty. She would not be another burden for him to bear.

She pulled the covers to her chin and stared into the cold dark bedroom, recalling the day they'd discovered they could both fit into the old copper bathtub. They'd subsequently explored the sensual properties of warm water on cool skin, and laughingly created whitecaps and sloshed soapy water all over the floor. Later that night they'd pored over the guest register they'd found in a cupboard drawer, smiling as the Larsons must have smiled at the messages travelers had left behind over the years. With a sense that they were preserving what they'd shared together, they scrawled their own message on the brittle, yellowed paper, then closed the book and made sweet, poignant love.

With her memories to warm her, Jo drifted into a fitful sleep. She was teetering on the edge of consciousness when Cooper's low, warning growl set her on edge. Her eyes slammed open. Her heart boomeranged inside her ribs. Without questioning why she was certain, she knew someone was in the house.

She lay very still. Listening for another sound, she tried to remember if she'd locked the door after Steve had left.

Willing herself to be calm and her bedsprings not to creak, she turned back the covers and rolled soundlessly to the floor. She groped under the bed, her fingers closing around the heavy steel of the long-barreled shotgun she kept loaded there. Rising shakily, she tiptoed on bare feet to her open bedroom door. Her fingers trembled as she tugged her flannel nightgown tighter against her throat and braved a hesitant step into the living room.

A tall, shadowy figure emerged out of the darkness just as she cleared the doorway.

She stifled a scream and raised the gun to her shoulder, taking a bead on what she hoped was his heart.

"You're as good as dead if you move," she warned him with wavering conviction. "Don't doubt it for an instant."

Every ounce of her blood careened through her body and pooled in her head. She was dizzy with fear as he stood stock-still, looming like a mountain in the darkness.

"You been watching those old gangster movies again, Red?" The familiar husky voice filled the dead silence.

Fighting disbelief and hope and an uncontrollable weakness in her knees, she stumbled to the wall and flicked on the light, then stared in heart-lurching shock at the glorious sight of Adam Dursky's cold-reddened nose and frosty gray eyes staring back at her from within the hood of his parka.

He flipped the hood back. "Hello, little girl."

His voice was as warm as the night was cold. His gaze swept hungrily across her face before veering to the shotgun.

"One way or the other," he finally said, "I wish you'd put me out of my misery. Shoot me or kiss me, or send me back out in the cold, but do something." His weak attempt at humor was laced with quiet desperation.

She didn't know whether to laugh or cry. She did both as she lowered the gun and launched herself into his open arms. "Adam!"

He buried his face in her hair and held her hard against him. But it wasn't enough. Prying her arms from around his neck, he unzipped his heavy jacket and drew her inside against his warmth. Knotting his hands in her hair, he dragged her head back so he could look into her eyes. "Lord, I've missed you."

"Don't talk," she whispered urgently, covering his face with her hands. She pulled his mouth down to hers. "Don't talk, just hold me." To her utter horror, she began to cry, small, breathless sobs at first, but they escalated to hard, wracking shudders that stole her strength and her control. "I've . . . m-missed you . . . missed you," she managed between gulps.

"I know, baby. I know." He held her like he'd never let her go. He rocked her until her trembling stopped, then scooped her in his arms and carried her to the sofa before the fire.

Shrugging out of his parka, he settled her onto his lap and brushed her hair from her tearstained cheeks.

"Better?" he asked, tucking her nightgown around her bare toes, then warming them with his hand.

She nodded. "I'm sorry. I don't know where that came from." She laughed sharply. "I don't know where *you* came from. How did you get here?"

He eased deeper into the sofa. For the first time, she noticed the lines of fatigue on his face. Exhausted as he was, she'd never seen a more beautiful sight.

"I came the first eight hundred miles by bus and the last thirty by the seat of my pants. I hired someone with a pickup when I got to International Falls. We four-wheeled it as far as the lake road, then snowmobiled the rest of the way in."

She had spent three months missing him. The reality of his presence in her living room was suddenly too much to accept at face value. "Why are you here?"

Adam filled his senses with her nearness. Several long moments passed before he cupped her face in his hands. "I'm here," he said, "because for too many nights I've had to be content only dreaming about green eyes the color of springtime when you're happy, fiery emeralds when you're not." His gaze drifted lovingly across her face. "Because for too long, I could only try to remember the feel of skin too soft to be real." He brushed his thumbs across her proud yet delicate cheekbones. Then he tunneled his long fingers through her hair as though he couldn't wait any longer to touch it. "I'm here because I couldn't go another day without filling my hands with spun gold."

She circled his wrists with her hands and pressed them against her cheeks. "I didn't know you were a poet," she said shakily, her eyes filled with wonder.

He smiled sheepishly. "I didn't either. But then I didn't know I was a lot of things until I found you . . . or until I lost you." He looked deep into her eyes. "Just so you'll know it's really me, let me put it this way." He paused and let a slow, sexy grin steal the last hint of chill from her heart and fill it with love. "I'm here because I'd gotten used to taking orders from a short, brassy redhead, because I miss your nasty little mouth, because of the way you looked in just my shirt . . ." His voice dropped to a low, husky rumble. "Because of the way you looked in just my socks."

She lowered her eyes.

A strong finger curled under her chin and brought her head up. "And I guess I'm just a sucker for your dog," he added, grinning as Cooper tried to squeeze up onto the couch beside them. But the humor left his eyes with his next breath. "I haven't been able to eat, or sleep, or think of anything but you, Red, since I left here."

She got lost in the love she saw in his eyes.

"I'm here, because without you, there's nothing

to try for. Because with you, I want to try everything.

"Jo." He murmured her name with so much tenderness, her heart ached. "I tried to stay away. I swear to God, I meant to leave you alone."

"Why?" The wonder in her question was peppered with pain. "I love you."

"You think I don't know that?"

All the hurt of the last three months balled into a fist in her stomach and materialized as anger. "It hurt so much when you left."

He growled and drew her to him. "I wanted to give you a chance. I wanted to do the right thing by you. And I tried. I couldn't stay away, though. The longer I stayed in that city, the more I realized what I'd left behind. I had come here to try to find some meaning to my life, then like a fool I left all the answers behind . . . with you."

"Your answers were always with you. Inside."

He closed his eyes and held her closer. "But it was you who made me feel things and want things I'd never thought I was entitled to have . . . and that scared the hell out of me."

She could feel his reservations. "So what made you decide you were entitled?"

"I'm not so sure I am."

"If that's the case," she said gently, "we're back where we started. Why are you here?"

"You're going to push this to the limit, aren't you?"

"Yes, I'm going to push, and pull, and scratch, and growl, if that's what it takes to keep you here. I want you with me without the worry that someday you'll be gone again. I need to know you've reached your own peace." She drew back and looked deep into his eyes. "And I want you to pay for the hell you put me through the past three months. Tell me exactly why you're here."

He kissed her deeply, sweetly. She melted into

his embrace, loving the feel of his arms around her, the taste of his mouth on her tongue.

"I'm here," he whispered against her lips, "because I love you and I need you and even though you'll never admit it, because I know you need me too. I want to spend the rest of my life with you, Joanna."

They were the sweetest words she'd ever heard. That a man such as this one would confess to needing her was the ultimate accolade. And he was so right. She did need him, desperately, completely.

He brushed away the tears tracking down her cheeks. "What do you think, Red?" he asked, smiling into her eyes. "Would you be in the market for an ex-cop and a Johnny-come-lately poet who wants to leave the world behind and spend the rest of his days under the thumb of a stubborn, mule-headed, independent little snip of a woman who doesn't have the good sense to come in out of the rain? Have you any need for a beat-up old veteran who can't row a boat or bait a line?"

"I have a need," she whispered as she eased off his lap and held out her hand. "One you can satisfy right now." She led him toward her bedroom.

"Wait." He left her just outside the door and returned with a package wrapped in bright paper. "I was going to put it under your tree." He nodded toward her bedroom. "But I don't want you to have to wait any longer. Go on, open it, but when you put it on, remember I bought it for you, not for me."

He kissed the bewildered smile from her lips and turned her gently toward the bedroom door. "Go."

Her hand shook as she lay the package on the bed. She plucked loose the red ribbon and tore aside the wrapping. Very carefully she removed the lid and folded back the rustling tissue paper, knowing before she saw it what she would find.

Delicate ivory lace trimmed the deep V neckline of a sheer silk nightgown. She touched it lovingly, then held the creamy fabric to her cheek for a moment before she tugged her old flannel nightgown over her head and replaced it with his gift.

The expensive silk caressed her body like water. She took a long look in her mirror. Would he notice the slight roundness of her tummy, the fullness of her breasts? Swallowing the lump in her throat, she turned and walked to the door.

He was standing by the fire staring into the flames, a distant look in his eyes. He'd taken off his shoes and socks. His shirt was unbuttoned and pulled free of his jeans. His head came up when she entered the room. She heard his indrawn breath, read the urgency in his eyes, and felt a matching need coil tight in her belly.

His gaze traveled from her shining hair down her silk-wrapped body, then back up to her face. "You are beautiful."

"So are you. Your leg has healed."

He nodded and peeled his shirt from his shoulders. "And you've got two good hands to love me." He tossed the shirt negligently on the sofa, then picked up the comforter that was folded across the arm of a nearby chair. "I'm going to miss zipping up your pants, though."

She smiled, suddenly shy with him.

"The first time I loved you was by firelight," he said huskily as he spread the thick blanket on the floor before the hearth. He knelt and held out his hand. "Come let me love you again. It's been far too long."

She went to him. His big hands pulled her near, circling her buttocks and drawing her against him. His mouth was hot and hungry against her stomach as she leaned over him, cloaking him in the curtain of her hair. The lean muscles of his shoulders felt like steel warmed by sun beneath her hands.

"To think," he whispered, "I'd given up on life."

She threaded her fingers through his hair and held him tight. "To think I'd given up on love."

He growled low in his throat and tugged on the silk with his teeth. "Can I take this damn thing off now?"

She laughed, a deep, self-assured woman's laugh, and joined him on her knees on the floor. With a sensual shrug, she slipped the fragile lace straps from her shoulders. He stripped the gown to her waist and bent his head to her bare breast.

"Nothing in the world tastes as good as this," he murmured, dragging his lips across her nipple until it grew rigid with desire. He wet it with his tongue, rimmed it lightly with his teeth, then suckled gently. It wasn't enough. Cupping her fullness with his palm, he lifted her, drawing her deep into his mouth.

"Sweet, sweet girl," he whispered, his breath drifting across her skin like summer heat. She shivered and arched against him as he drew out her pleasure, milking the anticipation until she cried his name.

"Tell me how much you need me," he demanded, pulling her with him until he lay on his back and she was draped across him. "Tell me!"

"I need you so much, I hurt," she said, matching his urgency. "Here." She lifted his hand to her mouth and kissed his palm. "Here." She guided his hand to her breast and pressed it there, leaving her own hand to ride on the back of his as he caressed her. "Here," she whispered breathlessly, her eyes glazed with longing as she lowered his hand to the part of her that was moist with wanting him. "Come inside me, Adam. I miss you being there."

He rolled her to her back and fit himself between the cradle of her thighs. He kissed her deeply, foraging into the silken heat of her mouth with explicit invitation before drawing back and looking into her eyes. "How can you be better, sweeter . . . even more than I remember?"

The unqualified love she saw in his eyes gave her courage.

"I *am* better." She framed his beloved face in her hands and held him still above her. "I *am* more, because I carry a part of you inside me. Adam . . . your doctors were wrong."

The fever in his eyes transformed to question, the question to disbelief, the disbelief to wonder.

He drew back, propping his weight on one elbow. His gaze swept her body from breast to belly. With the care of an artist handling spun glass, he cupped an ivory breast in his palm, weighing, fitting, comparing reality to memory. With awe, he skimmed his hand down her ribs to the slight protrusion of her stomach. He measured her waist with his hand, cupped his palm over her tummy.

She caught her lower lip between her teeth when his gaze found hers again. Her eyes misted over with tears as, like a slow sun at daybreak, a tentative, cautious light replaced the shadows in his eyes. "It's . . . not possible." The hope in his voice challenged his own denial.

She cupped his cheek in her palm. "Then my obstetrician is going to be a very disappointed man. He thinks he's going to deliver a baby in six months."

She would remember the look on his face for her lifetime. He kissed her gently, then closed his eyes and pressed his cheek to hers. For what seemed like an eternity he held her that way, his heart beating steadily against hers before he lowered his head to her stomach. He pressed his mouth to her belly in a long, reverent kiss, then rested his cheek on the warm, resilient flesh that harbored his child. She felt the moisture of his silent tears and rejoiced in the joy she had brought him.

"Introduce yourself to your child, Adam," she said gently. "We both need to get to know you again."

With infinite care, he entered her. He filled her slowly, as though he thought she might break, as though he would die if he hurt her, as though she were his world and his light and his reason for living. And he loved her ever so gently because she was all those things to him. All those things and more.

She was sitting on the sofa, her knees tucked under her chin, her toes buried deep in the cushion, when he woke up. Rolling over on his side, he propped his head on his palm and scowled sleepily at her.

"What are you doing up there?"

She smiled. "I'm watching you sleep."

"Why aren't you watching me sleep from down here where I can touch you?"

"Because if you touch me, I end up close to you and then I can only see your face. I wanted to see all of you."

"I want to see all of you too . . . but you've got that damn nightgown on again."

"This nightgown happens to be a gift from a very special man. And besides . . ." She gave him a sassy grin. "I like wearing it."

He reached out and took her foot in his hand, dragging it from the sofa cushion. "And I like taking it off. Come here."

When he had her where he wanted her, naked and spent beneath him, he brushed the damp hair back from her temples and feasted on the porcelain perfection of her face. "If I hadn't come back, were you going to tell me about the baby?"

She understood the anguish in his eyes and answered him truthfully. "I told myself I wouldn't. I told myself I wouldn't use the baby to get you to come back to me. And then, too, I hadn't thought that far ahead. It was such a shock. Don't get me wrong. I was thrilled. I *am* thrilled. I thought, if I couldn't have you, at least I could have a part of you. I wouldn't be alone anymore.

"But I was afraid, Adam. I didn't know how you would react if I told you. I couldn't bear it if you had felt trapped, or worse yet, if you thought it wasn't yours."

He swore softly. "You foolish, foolish girl. What would you have done by yourself?"

"I'd have done what I always do. I'd get by. And I did have an offer. Steve asked me to marry him."

"Steve," he murmured thoughtfully. "Did he know about the baby?"

"I had to talk to someone."

He pressed a kiss to her forehead. "I owe him for looking out for you, but I'll be damned if I'll forget that he tried to move in on my woman."

"No, Adam Dursky." She traced the line of his strong nose with her finger. "You won't be damned. You'll be blessed, and so will I as soon as I get your ring on my finger."

"And your ring in my nose?" he asked, sliding lower and teasing her nipple to an erect peak.

"I . . . ah, I think not. I wouldn't want anything to interfere with . . . ah—Adam! With what you do to me."

"It's only the beginning, Red," he promised, moving over her again. "There's not much else to do up here in the winter anyway, is there?"

"No." She sighed contentedly as he turned her over onto her tummy.

"How long do we have until spring?"

"Three or four months, unless—Adam, what are you doing?"

He nipped her left cheek lightly. "Just keeping the home fires burning, Red. Now relax and let this city boy show you the proper way to pass the time in the wilderness in the winter."

It wasn't until morning that he gave her the letter from her father.

He watched her read it, saw the tears gather. "It was him," she said quietly.

He nodded.

"But how?"

"Does the name Robert Hodges mean anything to you?"

"Yes. He was one of our regulars for years before Daddy lost the resort."

"Well, it seems he's on the board of directors of Dreamscape. Your father knew that. When I told him it looked like you'd lose the lodge to them in a bidding war, he contacted Hodges."

She stared at him in disbelief.

"It took a lot for him to make that call, Jo. But he did it. And whatever he said to Hodges must have been exactly the right thing, because Dreamscape backed out."

"I owe him."

"I think maybe he figures he owed you."

She was quiet for a very long time, then she went to her desk and took out a pen and paper.

"I think," she said, giving him a tentative, questioning look, "maybe it's time he came home."

She could see by the warmth and pride shining in his eyes that he agreed. "He'd like that."

Looking out over the lake, then back at the man who had shown her that love, when it's strong and true, could overcome any obstacle, she smiled. "I think I'd like that too."

THE EDITOR'S CORNER

What could be more romantic than weddings? Picture the bride in an exquisite gown. Imagine the handsome groom in a finely tailored tuxedo. Hear them promise "to have and to hold" each other forever. This is the perfect ending to courtship, the joyous ritual we cherish in our hearts. And next month, in honor of June brides, we present six fabulous LOVESWEPTs with beautiful brides and handsome grooms on the covers.

Leading the line-up is **HER VERY OWN BUTLER,** LOVESWEPT #552, another sure-to-please romance from Helen Mittermeyer. Single mom Drew Laughlin wanted a butler to help run her household, but she never expected a muscled, bronzed Hercules to apply. Rex Dakeland promised an old friend to check up on Drew and her children, but keeping his secret soon feels too much like spying. Once unexpected love ensnares them both, could he win her trust and be her one and only? A real treat, from one of romance's best-loved authors.

Gail Douglas pulls out all the stops in **ALL THE WAY,** LOVESWEPT #553. Jake Mallory and Brittany Thomas shared one fabulous night together, but he couldn't convince her it was enough to build their future on. Now, six months later, Jake is back from his restless wandering and sets out to prove to Brittany that he's right. It'll take fiery kisses and spellbinding charm to make her believe that the reckless nomad is finally ready to put down roots. Gail will win you over with this charming love story.

WHERE THERE'S A WILL . . . by Victoria Leigh, LOVESWEPT #554, is a sheer delight. Maggie Cooper plays a ditzy seductress on the ski slopes, only to prove to herself that she's sexy enough to kindle a man's desire. And boy, does she kindle Will Jackson's desire! He usually likes to do the hunting, but letting Maggie work her wiles on him is tantalizing fun. And after he's freed her from her doubts, he'll teach her to dare to love. There's a lot of wonderful verve and dash in this romance from talented Victoria.

Laura Taylor presents a very moving, very emotional love story in **DESERT ROSE,** LOVESWEPT #555. Emma Hamilton and David Winslow are strangers caught in a desperate situation, wrongfully imprisoned in a foreign country. Locked in adjacent cells, they whisper comfort to each other and reach through iron bars to touch hands. Love blossoms between them in that dark prison, a love strong enough to survive until fate finally brings them freedom. You'll cry and cheer for these memorable lovers. Bravo, Laura!

There's no better way to describe Deacon Brody than **RASCAL,** Charlotte Hughes's new LOVESWEPT, #556. He was once a country-music sensation, and he's never forgotten how hard he struggled to make it—or the woman who broke his heart. Losing Cody Sherwood sends him to Nashville determined to make her sorry she let him go, but when he sees her again, he realizes he's never stopped wanting her or the passion that burned so sweetly between them. Charlotte delivers this story with force and fire.

Please give a rousing welcome to Bonnie Pega and her first novel, **ONLY YOU,** LOVESWEPT #557. To efficiency expert Max Shore, organizing Caitlin Love's messy office is a snap compared to uncovering the sensual woman beneath her professional facade. A past pain has etched caution deep in her heart, and only Max can show her how to love again. This enchanting novel will show you why we're excited to have Bonnie writing for LOVESWEPT. Enjoy one of our New Faces of '92!

On sale this month from FANFARE are three marvelous novels. The historical romance **HEATHER AND VELVET** showcases the exciting talent of a rising star—Teresa Medeiros. Her marvelous touch for creating memorable characters and her exquisite feel for portraying passion and emotion shine in this grand adventure of love between a bookish orphan and a notorious highwayman known as the Dreadful Scot Bandit. Ranging from the storm-swept English countryside to the wild moors of Scotland, **HEATHER AND VELVET** has garnered the following praise from *New York Times* bestselling author Amanda Quick: "A terrific tale full of larger-than-life characters and thrilling romance." Teresa Medeiros—a name to watch for.

Lush, dramatic, and poignant, **LADY HELLFIRE** by Suzanne Robinson is an immensely thrilling historical romance. Its hero, Alexis de Granville, Marquess of Richfield, is a cold-blooded rogue whose tragic—and possibly violent—past has hardened his heart to love . . . until he melts at the fiery touch of Kate Grey's sensual embrace.

Anna Eberhardt, who writes short romances under the pseudonym Tiffany White, has been nominated for *Romantic Times*'s Career Achievement award for Most Sensual Romance in a series. In **WHISPERED HEAT,** she delivers a compelling contemporary novel of love lost, then regained. When Slader Reems is freed after five years of being wrongly imprisoned, he sets out to reclaim everything that was taken from him—including Lissa Jamison.

Also on sale this month, in the Doubleday hardcover edition, is **HIGHLAND FLAME** by Stephanie Bartlett, the stand-alone "sequel" to **HIGHLAND REBEL**. Catriona Galbaith, now a widow, is thrust into a new struggle—and the arms of a new love.

Happy reading!

With best wishes,

Nita Taublib

Nita Taublib
Associate Publisher
LOVESWEPT and FANFARE

FANFARE

On Sale in June

RAVISHED

☐ 29316-8 $4.99/5.99 in Canada

by Amanda Quick

New York Times bestselling author

Sweeping from a cozy seaside village to glittering London, this enthralling tale of a thoroughly mismatched couple poised to discover the rapture of love is Amanda Quick at her finest.

THE PRINCESS

29836-4 $5.99

☐ **by Celia Brayfield**

He is His Royal Highness, the Prince Richard, and wayward son of the House of Windsor. He has known many women, but only three understand him, and only one holds the key to unlock the mysteries of his heart.

SOMETHING BLUE

29814-3 $5.99/6.99 in Canada

☐ **by Ann Hood**

author of SOMEWHERE OFF THE COAST OF MAINE

"An engaging, warmly old fashioned story of the perils and endurance of romance, work, and friendship." -- The Washington Post

SOUTHERN NIGHTS

☐ 29815-1 $4.99/5.99 in Canada

by Sandra Chastain,

Helen Mittermeyer, and Patricia Potter

Sultry, caressing, magnolia-scented breezes. . .sudden, fierce thunderstorms. . .nights of beauty and enchantment. In three original novellas, favorite LOVESWEPT authors present the many faces of summer and unexpected love.

☐ Please send me the books I have checked above I am enclosing $ ______ (add $2.50 to cover postage and handling). Send check or money order, no cash or C. O. D.'s please.

Mr / Ms ______________________

Address ______________________

City/ State/ Zip ______________________

Send order to: Bantam Books, Dept. FN, 2451 S. Wolf Rd., Des Plaines, IL 60018

Allow four to six weeks for delivery

Prices and availability subject to change without notice FN 50 6/92

Look for these books at your bookstore or use this form to order